Aleph

Paulo Coelho

Aleph

Translated from the Portuguese by
Margaret Jull Costa

HarperCollins*Publishers*

HarperCollins*Publishers*
77–85 Fulham Palace Road,
Hammersmith, London W6 8JB

www.harpercollins.co.uk

First published by HarperCollins*Publishers* 2011

1 3 5 7 9 10 8 6 4 2

A catalogue record of this book is
available from the British Library

978-0-00-745609-3

Printed and bound in India by
Thomson Press India Ltd.

O Mary, conceived without sin,
pray for those who turn to you.
Amen.

A certain nobleman went into a far country to
receive for himself a kingdom, and to return.

Luke 19:12

For J. who keeps me walking,

S. J. who continues to protect me,

Hilal, for her words of forgiveness in the
church in Novosibirsk.

The Aleph was about two to three centimetres in diameter, but all of cosmic space was there, with no diminution in size. Each thing was infinite, because I could clearly see it from every point on the universe.

Jorge Luis Borges, 'The Aleph'

Thou knowest all – I cannot see.
I trust I shall not live in vain,
I know that we shall meet again
In some divine eternity.

Oscar Wilde, 'The True Knowledge'

King of My Kingdom

O h no, not another ritual! Not another invocation intended to make the invisible forces manifest in the visible world! What has that got to do with the world we live in today? Graduates leave university and can't find a job. Old people reach retirement and have almost nothing to live on. Grown-ups have no time to dream, struggling from nine to five to support their family and pay for their children's education, always bumping up against the thing we all know as 'harsh reality'.

The world has never been as divided as it is now, what with religious wars, genocides, a lack of respect for the planet, economic crises, depression, poverty, with everyone wanting instant solutions to at least some of the world's problems or their own. And things only look bleaker as we head into the future.

What am I doing here, trying to make my way in a spiritual tradition whose roots are in the remote past, far from all the challenges of the present moment?

* * *

Along with J., whom I call my Master, although I'm beginning to have doubts about that, I am walking towards the sacred oak tree, which, for more than five hundred years, has stood there impassively contemplating humanity's woes, its one concern being to surrender its leaves in winter and recover them in spring.

I can't stand to write any more about my relationship with J., my guide in the Tradition. I have dozens of diaries full of notes of our conversations, which I never bother to re-read. Since our first meeting in Amsterdam, in 1982, I have learned and unlearned how to live hundreds of times. Whenever J. teaches me something new, I think that perhaps this will be the last step required to reach the top of the mountain, the note that justifies a whole symphony, the word that sums up an entire book. I go through a period of euphoria, which gradually dissipates. Some things stay for ever, but most of the exercises, practices and teachings end up disappearing down a black hole. Or so it seems.

The ground is wet. It occurs to me that my trainers, meticulously washed two days before, will soon be covered in mud again, however carefully I tread. My search for wisdom, peace of mind and an awareness of realities visible and invisible has become routine and pointless. I began my apprenticeship in magic when I was twenty-two. I followed various paths, walked along the very edge of the abyss for many years, slipped and fell, gave up and started all over again. I imagined that, by the time I reached the age of fifty-nine, I would be close to paradise and to the absolute peace I thought I could see in the smiles of Buddhist monks.

In fact, I seem to be further from achieving that than ever. I'm not at peace; now and then I go through periods of inner conflict that can persist for months; and the times when I immerse myself in some magical reality last only seconds, just long enough to know that another world exists and long enough to leave me frustrated because I can't absorb everything I learn.

We arrive.

When the ritual is over, I'll have a serious talk with him. We both place our hands on the trunk of the sacred oak.

J. says a Sufi prayer:

'O God, when I listen to the voices of animals, the sounds of trees, the murmurings of water, the singing of birds, the whistling of the wind or the boom of thunder, I see in them evidence of Your unity; I feel that You are supreme power, omniscience, supreme knowledge and supreme justice.

'I recognise You, O God, in the trials I am going through. May Your pleasure be my pleasure too. May I be Your joy, the joy that a Father feels for a son. And may I think of You calmly and with determination, even when I find it hard to say I love You.'

Usually, at this point, I would feel – for only a fraction of a second, but that's always enough – the One Presence that moves the Sun and the Earth and ensures that the stars remain in their places. But I don't feel like talking to the Universe today, I just want the man at my side to give me the answers I need.

He removes his hands from the tree trunk, and I do the same. He smiles at me, and I return his smile. We make our way, in silence, unhurriedly, back to my house, where we sit on the verandah and drink coffee, still without talking.

I look at the huge tree in the middle of my garden, with a ribbon tied round its trunk, placed there after a dream I had. I am in the hamlet of Saint Martin, in the French Pyrenees, in a house I now regret having bought, because it has ended up owning me, demanding my presence whenever possible, because it needs someone to look after it, to keep its energy alive.

'I can't evolve any further,' I say, falling, as always, into the trap of being the first to speak. 'I think I've reached my limit.'

'That's funny. I've been trying all my life to find out what my limits are and have never reached them yet. But then my universe doesn't really help, it keeps expanding and won't allow me to know it entirely,' says J. provocatively.

He's being ironic, but I keep talking.

'Why did you come here today? To try and convince me that I'm wrong, as usual? You can say what you like, but words won't change anything. I'm not happy.'

'That's exactly why I came. I've been aware of what's been going on for some time now, but there is always a right moment to act,' says J., picking up a pear from the table and turning it over in his hands. 'If we had spoken before, you would not have been ripe. If we were to talk later, you would have rotted.' He bites into the pear, savouring the taste. 'Perfect. The right moment.'

'I'm filled with doubt, especially about my faith,' I say.

'Good. It's doubt that drives a man onward.'

The usual apt responses and images, but they're not working today.

'I'm going to tell you what you feel,' J. says. 'You feel that nothing you have learned has put down roots, that while you're capable of entering the magical universe, you cannot remain submerged in it, you feel that all of this may be nothing but a fantasy dreamed up by people to fend off their fear of death.'

My questions go deeper than that; they are doubts about my faith. I have only one certainty: there exists a parallel spiritual universe that impinges on the world in which we live. Apart from that, everything else seems absurd to me – sacred books, revelations, guides, manuals, ceremonies ... And, what is worse, they appear to have no lasting effects.

'I'm going to tell you what I once felt,' J. adds. 'When I was young, I was dazzled by all the things life could offer me. I thought I was capable of achieving all of them. When I got married, I had to choose just one path, because I needed to support the woman I love and my children. When I was forty-five and a highly successful executive, I saw my children grow up and leave home, and I thought that, from then on, everything would be a mere repetition of what I had already experienced. That was when my spiritual search began. I'm a disciplined man and I put all my energies into that. I went through periods of enthusiasm and unbelief, until I reached the stage you are at now.'

'Look, J., despite all my efforts, I still can't honestly say that I feel closer to God and to myself,' I tell him, with barely concealed exasperation.

'That's because, like everyone else on the planet, you believed that time would teach you to grow closer to God. But time doesn't teach; it merely brings us a sense of weariness and of growing older.'

The oak tree in my garden appears to be looking at me now. It must be more than four hundred years old, and the only thing it has learned is to stay in one place.

'Why did we go and perform that ritual around that other oak tree? How does that help us become better human beings?'

'Precisely because most people don't perform rituals around oak trees any more, and because by performing apparently absurd rituals, you get in touch with something deep in your soul, in the oldest part of yourself, the part closest to the origin of everything.'

That's true. I had asked a question to which I already knew the answer and received the answer I was expecting. I should make better use of his company.

'It's time to leave,' says J. abruptly.

I look at the clock. I tell him that the airport is nearby and that we can continue talking for a while longer.

'That isn't what I mean. When I went through what you're experiencing now, I found the answer in something that had happened before I was born. That's what I'm suggesting you do now.'

Reincarnation? But he had always discouraged me from visiting past lives.

'I've been back into the past already. I learned how to do that before I met you. We've talked before about how I saw two incarnations, one as a French writer in the nineteenth century and one—'

'Yes, I know.'

'I made mistakes then that I can't put right now. And you told me never to go back again, because it would only increase my sense of guilt. Travelling to past lives is like making a hole in the floor and letting the flames of the fire in the apartment below scorch and burn the present.'

J. throws what remains of his pear to the birds in the garden and looks at me with some irritation.

'If you don't stop spouting such nonsense, I might start believing that you're right and that you really haven't learned anything during the twenty-four years we've been together.'

I know what he means. In magic – and in life – there is only the present moment, the NOW. You can't measure time the way you measure the distance between two points. 'Time' doesn't pass. We human beings have enormous difficulty in focusing on the present; we're always thinking about what we did, about how we could have done it better, about the consequences of our actions, and why we didn't act as we should have. Or else we think about the future, about what we're going to do tomorrow, what precautions we should take, what dangers await us around the next corner, how to avoid what we don't want and how to get what we have always dreamed of.

J. takes up the conversation again.

'Right here and now, you are beginning to wonder: is there really something wrong? Yes, there is. But at this precise moment, you also realise that you can change your future by bringing the past into the present. Past and future only exist in our mind. The present moment, though, is outside of time, it's Eternity. In India they use the word "karma" for lack of any better term. But it's a concept that's rarely given a proper explanation. It isn't

8

what you did in the past that will affect the present. It's what you do in the present that will redeem the past and thereby change the future.'

'So …'

He pauses, becoming increasingly irritated at my inability to grasp what he's trying to explain to me.

'There's no point sitting here, using words that mean nothing. Go and experiment. It's time you got out of here. Go and re-conquer your kingdom, which has grown corrupted by routine. Stop repeating the same lesson, because you won't learn anything new that way.'

'It's not routine that's the problem. I'm simply not happy.'

'That's what I mean by routine. You think that you exist because you're unhappy. Other people exist merely as a function of their problems and spend all their time talking compulsively about their children, their husband, school, work, friends. They never stop to think: I'm here. I am the result of everything that happened and will happen, but I'm here. If I did something wrong, I can put it right or at least ask forgiveness. If I did something right, that leaves me happier and more connected with the now.'

J. takes a deep breath, then concludes:

'You're not here any more. You've got to leave in order to return to the present.'

*   *   *

9

It was as I had feared. For a while now, he has been dropping hints that it was time I set off on the third sacred
road. My life has changed a lot since the far-off year of
1986, when my pilgrimage to Santiago de Compostela
brought me face to face with my destiny, or 'God's plan'.
Three years later, I followed the so-called Road to Rome,
in the area where we were now; it was a painful, tedious
process lasting seventy days, and which involved me
enacting, each morning, all the absurd things I had
dreamed about the night before (I remember standing
at a bus stop for four whole hours, during which nothing of any importance happened).

Since then, I have done everything that my work
demanded of me. After all, it was my choice and my
blessing. I started travelling like a mad thing. The great
lessons I learned had been precisely those that my journeys had taught me.

Well, the truth is, I've always travelled like a mad thing,
ever since I was young. Recently, though, I seem to be
spending my life in airports and hotels, and any sense of
adventure has rapidly given way to profound tedium.
When I complained that I never stayed in one place for
very long, people were horrified: 'But it's great to travel.
I wish I had the money to do what you're doing!'

Travel is never a matter of money, but of courage. I
spent a large part of my youth travelling the world as a
hippie, and what money did I have then? None. I barely
had enough to pay for my fare, but I still consider those

to have been the best years of my youth: eating badly, sleeping in train stations, unable to communicate because I didn't know the language, being forced to depend on others just for somewhere to spend the night.

After weeks on the road, listening to a language you don't understand, using a currency whose value you don't comprehend, walking down streets you've never walked down before, you discover that your old 'I', along with everything you ever learned, is absolutely no use at all in the face of those new challenges, and you begin to realise that, buried deep in your unconscious mind, there is someone much more interesting and adventurous and more open to the world and to new experiences.

Then there comes a day when you say: 'Enough!'

'Enough! Travelling, for me, has become just a monotonous routine.'

'No, it's not enough, it never will be,' says J. 'Our life is a constant journey, from birth to death. The landscape changes, the people change, our needs change, but the train keeps moving. Life is the train, not the station. And what you're doing now isn't travelling, it's just changing countries, which is completely different.'

I shake my head.

'It won't help. If I need to put right a mistake in another life and I'm deeply aware of that mistake, I can do that here. In that prison cell, I was just obeying the orders of someone who seemed to know God's will: you. Besides, I've already asked forgiveness of at least four people.'

'But you've never found the nature of the curse placed on you.'

'You were cursed too at the time. Did you find out what it was?'

'Yes, I did. And I can guarantee that it was far harsher than yours. You committed just one cowardly deed, while I acted unfairly many times. But that discovery freed me.'

'If I need to travel in time, why do I have to travel in space as well?'

J. laughs. 'Because we all have the possibility of redemption, but for that to happen, we have to seek out the people we harmed and ask their forgiveness.'

'So where should I go? To Jerusalem?'

'I don't know. Wherever you are committed to going. Find out what you have left unfinished and complete the task. God will guide you, because everything you ever experienced or will experience is in the here and now. The world is being created and destroyed in this very moment. Whoever you met will reappear, whoever you lost will return. Don't betray the grace that was bestowed on you. Understand what is going on inside you and you will understand what is going on inside everyone else. Don't imagine that I came to bring peace. I came with a sword.'

I'm standing in the rain shivering, and my first thought is, I'm going to catch the flu. I console myself by thinking that every doctor I've ever met has assured me that flu is caused by a virus, not by drops of water.

I can't stay in the here and now, my head is whirling. Where should I aim for? Where should I go? And what if I don't recognise the people on my path? That must have happened before and is bound to happen again; if it hadn't, my soul would be at peace.

After fifty-nine years of living with myself, I can predict at least some of my reactions. When I first met J., his words seemed filled with a light much brighter than he himself. I accepted everything without question; I walked fearlessly ahead and never once regretted it. But time passed, we got to know each other and with familiarity came habit. He had never let me down in any way, but I couldn't see him now with quite the same eyes. Even though, out of duty, I had to obey his words – which I would have done gladly in September of 1992, ten years after I met him – I no longer did so with the same conviction.

I am wrong. It was my choice to follow this magical Tradition, so why question it now. I'm free to abandon it whenever I wish, but something drives me on. He's probably right, but I've got used to the life I lead and I don't need any more challenges. I need peace.

I should be a happy man: I'm successful in my chosen, highly competitive profession; I've been married for twenty-seven years to the woman I love; I enjoy good health; I live surrounded by people I can trust; I'm always greeted with affection by my readers when I meet them in the street. There was a time when that was enough, but these last two years, nothing seems to satisfy me.

Is it just a passing anxiety? Won't it be enough just to say the usual prayers, respect nature as if it were the voice of God and contemplate the beauty around me? Why go forward, if I'm convinced that I've reached my limit?

WHY CAN'T I BE LIKE MY FRIENDS?

The rain is falling ever harder and all I can hear is the sound of the water. I'm drenched, but I can't move. I don't want to leave because I don't know where to go. J. is right. I'm lost. If I really had reached my limit, this feeling of guilt and frustration would have passed, but it's still there. Fear and trembling. When a sense of dissatisfaction persists, that means it was placed there by God for one reason only: you need to change everything and move forward.

I've been through this before. Whenever I refused to follow my fate, something very hard to bear would happen in my life. And that is my great fear at the moment, that some tragedy will occur. Tragedy always brings about radical change in our lives, a change that

14

is associated with the same principle: loss. When faced by any loss, there's no point in trying to recover what has been, it's best to take advantage of the large space that opens up before us and fill it with something new. In theory, every loss is for our good; in practice, though, that is when we question the existence of God and ask ourselves, 'What did I do to deserve this?'

Lord, preserve me from tragedy and I will follow Your desires.

The moment I think this, there is a great crack of thunder and the sky is lit up by a flash of lightning.

Again, fear and trembling. A sign. Here I am trying to persuade myself that I always give the best of myself and nature is telling me exactly the opposite: anyone truly committed to life never stops walking. Heaven and earth are meeting in a storm which, when it's over, will leave the air purer and the fields fertile, but before that happens, houses will be destroyed, centuries-old trees will topple, paradises will be flooded.

A yellow shape approaches.

I surrender myself to the rain. There's more lightning, but my feeling of helplessness is being replaced by something positive, as if my soul were gradually being washed clean by the water of forgiveness.

Bless and you will be blessed.

The words emerge naturally from me – a wisdom I didn't know I had, which I know does not belong to me, but which appears sometimes and stops me doubting everything I have learned over the years.

My great problem is this: despite such moments, I continue to doubt.

The yellow shape is there before me. It's my wife, wearing one of the garish capes we use when we go walking in remote parts of the mountains. If we get lost, we'll be easy to find.

'Have you forgotten that we're going out to supper tonight?'

No, I haven't forgotten. I abandon universal metaphysics, in which thunder claps are the voices of the gods, and return to the reality of a provincial town and a supper of good wine, roast lamb and the cheerful conversation of friends, who will tell us about their recent adventures on their Harley-Davidson. I go back home to change my clothes and give my wife a brief summary of my conversation with J. that afternoon.

'Did he tell you where you should go?' she asks.

'He told me to make a commitment.'

'And is that so very hard? Stop being so difficult. You're acting like an old man.'

Hervé and Véronique have invited two other guests, a middle-aged French couple. One of them is introduced as a 'clairvoyant', whom they met in Morocco.

The man seems neither pleasant nor unpleasant, merely absent. Then, in the middle of supper, as if he had entered a kind of trance, he says to Véronique:

'Be careful when driving. You're going to have an accident.'

I find this remark in the worst possible taste, because if Véronique takes it seriously, her fear will end up attracting negative energy and then things really might turn out as predicted.

'How interesting,' I say, before anyone else can react. 'You are presumably capable of travelling in time, back into the past and forward into the future. I was speaking about just that with a friend this afternoon.'

'When God allows me to, I can see. I know who each of the people around this table was, is and will be. I don't understand my gift, but I long ago learned to accept it.'

The conversation should be about the trip to Sicily with friends who share a passion for classic Harley-Davidsons, but suddenly it seems to have taken a dangerous turn into areas I don't want to enter right now. A case of synchronicity.

It's my turn to speak:

'You also know, then, that God only allows us to see such things when he wants something to change.'

I turn to Véronique and say, 'Just take care. When something on the astral plane is placed on the earthly plane, it loses a lot of its force. In other words, I'm almost sure there will be no accident.'

Véronique offers everyone more wine. She thinks that the Moroccan clairvoyant and I are on a collision course. This isn't the case; the man really can 'see' and that frightens me. I'll talk to Hervé about it afterwards.

The man barely looks at me; he still has the absent air of someone who has unwittingly entered another dimension and now has a duty to communicate what he is experiencing. He wants to tell me something, but chooses, instead, to turn to my wife.

'The soul of Turkey will give your husband all the love she possesses, but she will spill his blood before she reveals what it is she is seeking.'

Another sign confirming that I should not travel now, I think, knowing full well that we always try to interpret things in accordance with what we want and not as they are.

Chinese Bamboo

Sitting in this train travelling from Paris to London, on my way to the Book Fair, is a blessing to me. Whenever I visit England, I remember 1977, when I left my job with a Brazilian recording company determined, from then on, to make my living as a writer. I rented a flat in Bassett Road, made various friends, studied vampirology, discovered the city on foot, fell in love, saw every film being shown and, before a year had passed, I was back in Rio, incapable of writing a single line.

This time I will only be staying in London for three days. There will be a signing session, meals in Indian and Lebanese restaurants, and conversations in the hotel lobby about books, bookshops and authors. I have no plans to return to my house in Saint Martin until the end of the year. From London I will get a flight back to Rio, where I can again hear my mother tongue spoken in the streets, drink acai juice every night and gaze tirelessly out of my window at the most beautiful view in the world: Copacabana beach.

*　　*　　*

Shortly before we arrive, a young man enters the carriage carrying a bunch of roses and starts looking around him. How odd, I think, I've never seen flower-sellers on Eurostar before.

'I need twelve volunteers,' he says. 'Each person will carry a single rose and present it to the woman who is the love of my life and whom I'm going to ask to marry me.'

Several people volunteer, including me, although, in the end, I'm not one of the chosen twelve. Nevertheless, when the train pulls into the station, I decide to follow the other volunteers. The young man points to a girl on the platform. One by one, the passengers hand her their red roses. Finally, he declares his love for her, everyone applauds, and the young woman turns scarlet with embarrassment. Then the couple kiss and go off, their arms around each other.

One of the stewards says:

'That's the most romantic thing I've seen in all the time I've been working here.'

The scheduled book-signing lasts nearly five hours, but it fills me with positive energy and makes me wonder why I've been in such a state all these months. If my spiritual progress seems to have met an insurmountable barrier, perhaps I just need to be patient. I have seen and felt things that very few of the people around me will have seen and felt.

Aleph

Before setting out to London, I visited the little chapel in Barbazan-Debat. There I asked Our Lady to guide me with her love and help me identify the signs that will lead me back to myself. I know that I am in all the people surrounding me, and that they are in me. Together we write the Book of Life, our every encounter determined by fate and our hands joined in the belief that we can make a difference in this world. Everyone contributes a word, a sentence, an image, but in the end, it all makes sense: the happiness of one becomes the joy of all.

We will always ask ourselves the same questions. We will always need to be humble enough to accept that our heart knows why we are here. Yes, it's difficult to talk to your heart, and perhaps it isn't even necessary. We simply have to trust and follow the signs and live our Personal Legend; sooner or later, we will realise that we are all part of something, even if we can't understand rationally what that something is. They say that in the second before our death, each of us understands the real reason for our existence and out of that moment Heaven or Hell is born.

Hell is when we look back during that fraction of a second and know that we wasted an opportunity to dignify the miracle of life. Paradise is being able to say at that moment: 'I made some mistakes, but I wasn't a coward. I lived my life and did what I had to do.'

However, there's no need to anticipate my particular hell and keep going over and over the fact that I can make no further progress in what I understand to be my 'Spiritual Quest'. It's enough that I keep trying. Even those who didn't do all they could have done have already been forgiven; they had their punishment while they were alive by being unhappy when they could have been living in peace and harmony. We are all redeemed and free to follow the path that has no beginning and will have no end.

I haven't brought anything with me to read. While I'm waiting to join my Russian publishers for supper, I leaf through one of those magazines that are always to be found in hotel rooms. I skim-read an article about Chinese bamboo. Apparently, once the seed has been sown, you see nothing for about five years apart from a tiny shoot. All the growth takes place underground, where a complex root system reaching upwards and outwards is being established. Then, at the end of the fifth year, the bamboo suddenly shoots up to a height of 25 metres. What a tedious subject! I decide to go downstairs and watch the comings and goings in the lobby.

I have a cup of coffee while I wait. Mônica, my agent and my best friend, joins me at my table. We talk about things of no importance. She's clearly tired after a day spent dealing with people from the book world and monitoring the book-signing over the phone with my British publisher.

We started working together when she was only twenty. She was a fan of my work and convinced that a Brazilian writer could be successfully translated and published outside Brazil. She abandoned her studies in chemical engineering in Rio, moved to Spain with her boyfriend and went round knocking on publishers' doors and writing letters, telling them that they really needed to read my work.

When this brought no results at all, I went to the small town in Catalonia where she was living, bought her a coffee and advised her to give the whole thing up and think about her own life and future. She refused and said that she couldn't go back to Brazil a failure. I tried to persuade her that she hadn't failed; after all, she had shown herself capable of surviving (by delivering leaflets and working as a waitress) as well as having had the unique experience of living abroad. Mônica would still not give up. I left that café in the firm belief that she was throwing her life away, but that I would never be able to make her change her mind because she was too stubborn. Six months later, the situation had changed completely, and six months after that, she had earned enough money to buy an apartment.

She believed in the impossible and, for that reason, won a battle that everyone, including myself, considered to be lost. That is what marks out the warrior: the knowledge that willpower and courage are not the same thing. Courage can attract fear and adulation, but willpower requires patience and commitment. Men and women with immense willpower are generally solitary types and give off a kind of coolness. Many people mistakenly think that Mônica is rather a cold person, when nothing could be further from the truth. In her heart there burns a secret fire, as intense as it was when we met in that Catalonian café. Despite all she has achieved, she's as enthusiastic as ever.

Just as I'm about to recount my recent conversation with J., my two publishers from Bulgaria come into the lobby. A lot of people involved in the Book Fair are staying in the same hotel. We talk about this and that, then Mônica turns the conversation to the subject of my books. Eventually, one of the publishers looks at me and asks the standard question:

'So when are you going to visit our country?'

'Next week if you can organise it. All I ask is a party after the afternoon signing session.'

They both look at me aghast.

Chinese Bamboo!

Mônica is staring at me in horror as she says:

'We'd better look at the diary …'

'… but I'm sure I can be in Sofia next week,' I burst in, adding in Portuguese: 'I'll explain later.'

Mônica sees that I'm serious, but the publishers are still unsure. They ask if I wouldn't prefer to wait a little, so that they can mount a proper promotion campaign.

'Next week,' I say again. 'Otherwise we'll have to leave it for another occasion.'

Only then do they realise that I'm serious. They turn to Mônica for more details. And at that precise moment my Spanish publisher arrives. The conversation at the table breaks off, introductions are made, and the usual question is asked:

'So, when are you coming back to Spain?'

'Straight after my visit to Bulgaria.'

'When will that be?'

'In two weeks' time. We can arrange a book-signing in Santiago de Compostela and another in the Basque Country, followed by a party to which some of my readers could be invited.'

The Bulgarian publishers start to look uneasy again, and Mônica gives a strained smile.

'Make a commitment!' J. had said.

The lobby is starting to fill up. At all such fairs, whether they're promoting books or heavy machinery, the professionals tend to stay in the same two or three hotels, and most deals are sealed in hotel lobbies or at suppers like the one due to take place tonight. I greet all the publishers and accept any invitations that begin with the question 'When are you going to visit our country?' I try to keep them talking for as long as possible to avoid Mônica asking me what on earth is going on. All she can do is note down in her diary the various visits I'm committing myself to.

At one point, I break off my discussion with an Arab publisher to find out how many visits I've arranged.

'Look, you're putting me in a very awkward position,' she replies in Portuguese, sounding very irritated.

'How many?'

'Six countries in five weeks. These fairs are for publishing professionals, you know, not writers. You don't have to accept any invitations, I take care of—'

Just then my Portuguese publisher arrives, so we can't continue this private conversation. When he doesn't say anything beyond the usual small talk, I ask the question myself:

'Aren't you going to invite me to Portugal?'

He admits that he overheard my conversation with Mônica.

'I'm not joking,' I say. 'I'd really love to do a book-signing in Guimarães and another in Fátima.'

'As long as you don't cancel at the last moment.'

'I won't cancel, I promise.'

He agrees, and Mônica adds Portugal to the diary: another five days. Finally, my Russian publishers – a man and a woman – come over and we say hello. Mônica gives a sigh of relief. Now she can drag me off to the restaurant.

While we're waiting for the taxi, she draws me to one side.

'Have you gone mad?'

'Oh, I went mad years ago. Do you know anything about Chinese bamboo? It apparently spends five years as a little shoot, using that time to develop its root system. And then, from one moment to the next, it puts on a spurt and grows up to twenty-five metres high.'

'And what has that got to do with the act of insanity I've just witnessed?'

'Later on, I'll tell you about the conversation I had a month ago with J. What matters now, though, is that this is precisely what has been happening to me: I've invested work, time and effort; I tried to encourage my personal growth with love and dedication, but nothing happened. Nothing happened for years.'

'What do you mean "nothing happened"? Have you forgotten who you are?'

The taxi arrives. The Russian publisher opens the door for Mônica.

'I'm talking about the spiritual side of my life. I think I'm like that Chinese bamboo plant and that my fifth year has just arrived. It's time for me to start growing again. You asked me if I'd gone mad and I answered with a joke. But the fact is, I have been going mad. I was beginning to believe that nothing I had learned had put down any roots.'

For a fraction of a second, immediately after the arrival of my Bulgarian publishers, I had felt J.'s presence at my side and only then did I understand his words, although the insight itself had come to me during a moment of boredom, after leafing through a magazine on gardening. My self-imposed exile, which, on the one hand, had helped me discover important truths about myself, had another serious side-effect: the vice of solitude. My universe had become limited to a few friends locally, to answering letters and emails and to the illusion that the rest of my time was mine alone. I was, in short, leading a life without any of the inevitable problems that arise from living with other people, from human contact.

Is that what I'm looking for? A life without challenges? But where is the pleasure in looking for God outside people?

I know many who have done just that. I once had a serious and at the same time comical talk with a Buddhist nun, who had spent twenty years alone in a cave in Nepal. I asked her what she had achieved. 'Spiritual orgasm,' she replied, to which I replied that there were far easier ways to achieve orgasm.

I could never follow that path; it's simply not on my horizon. I cannot and could not spend the rest of my life in search of spiritual orgasms or contemplating the oak tree in my garden, waiting for wisdom to descend. J. knows this and encouraged me to make this journey so that I would understand that my path is reflected in the eyes of others and that, if I want to find myself, I need that map.

Aleph

I apologise to the Russian publishers and say that I need to finish a conversation with Mônica in Portuguese. I start by telling her a story:

'A man stumbles and falls into a deep hole. He asks a passing priest to help him out. The priest blesses him and walks on. Hours later, a doctor comes by. The man asks for help, but the doctor merely studies his injuries from afar, writes him a prescription and tells him to buy the medicine from the nearest pharmacy. Finally, a complete stranger appears. Again, the man asks for help, and the stranger jumps into the hole. "Now what are we going to do?" says the man. "Now both of us are trapped down here." To which the stranger replies: "No we're not. I'm from around here and I know how to get out."'

'Meaning?' asks Mônica.

'That I need strangers like that,' I explain. 'My roots are ready, but I'll only manage to grow with the help of others. Not just you or J. or my wife, but people I've never met. I'm sure of that. That's why I asked for a party to be held after the book-signings.'

'You're never satisfied, are you?' Mônica says in a tone of complaint.

'That's why you love me so much,' I say with a smile.

In the restaurant, we speak about all kinds of things; we celebrate a few successes and try to refine certain details. I have to stop myself from interfering, because

Mônica is in charge of everything to do with publishing. At one point, though, the same question is asked:

'And when will Paulo be visiting Russia?'

Mônica starts explaining that my diary has suddenly got very crowded and that I have a series of commitments starting next week. I break in:

'You know, I have long cherished a dream, which I've tried to realise twice before and failed. If you can help me achieve my dream, I'll come to Russia.'

'What dream is that?'

'To cross the whole of Russia by train and end up at the Pacific Ocean. We could stop at various places along the way for signings. That way we would be showing our respect for all those readers who could never make it to Moscow.'

My publisher's eyes light up with joy. He had just been talking about the increasing difficulties of distribution in a country so vast that it has nine different time zones.

'A very romantic, very Chinese bamboo idea,' laughs Mônica, 'but not very practical. As you well know, I wouldn't be able to go with you because I have my son to look after now.'

The publisher, however, is enthusiastic. He orders his fifth coffee of the night, says that he'll take care of everything, that Mônica's assistant can stand in for her, and that she needn't worry about a thing, it will all be fine.

I thus fill up my diary with two whole months of travelling, leaving along the way a lot of very happy, but very stressed-out people who are going to have to organise everything at lightning speed; a friend and agent who is now looking at me with affection and respect; and a teacher who isn't here, but who knows that I've now made a commitment, even though I didn't understand what he meant at the time. It's a cold night and I choose to walk back alone to the hotel, feeling rather frightened at what I've done, but happy too, because there's no turning back.

That is what I wanted. If I believe I will win, then victory will believe in me. No life is complete without a touch of madness, or to use J.'s words, what I need to do is to re-conquer my kingdom. If I can understand what's going on in the world, I can understand what's going on inside myself.

At the hotel, there is a message from my wife, saying that she's been trying to contact me and asking me to phone her as soon as possible. My heart starts pounding, because she rarely phones me when I'm travelling. I return her call at once. The seconds between each ring seem like an eternity.

Finally, she picks up the phone.

'Véronique has had a serious car accident, but, don't worry, she's not in any danger,' she says nervously.

I ask if I can phone Véronique now, but she says not. She's still in hospital.

'Do you remember that clairvoyant?' she asks.

Of course I do! He made a prediction about me as well. We hang up and I immediately phone Mônica's room. I ask if, by any chance, I've arranged a visit to Turkey.

'Can't you even remember which invitations you accepted?'

No, I say. I was in a strange state of euphoria when I started saying 'Yes' to all those publishers.

'But you do remember the commitments you've taken on, don't you? There's still time to cancel, if you want to.'

I tell her that I'm perfectly happy with the commitments, that's not the problem. It's too late to start explaining about the clairvoyant, the predictions, and Véronique's accident. I ask Mônica again if I have arranged a visit to Turkey.

'No,' she says. 'The Turkish publishers are staying in a different hotel. Otherwise ...'

We both laugh.

I can sleep easy.

The Stranger's Lantern

Almost two months of travelling, of pilgrimage. My joy in life has returned, but I lie awake all night wondering if that sense of joy will stay with me when I return home. Am I doing what I need to do to make the Chinese bamboo grow? I've been to seven countries, met my readers, had fun and temporarily driven away the depression that was threatening to engulf me, but something tells me that I still haven't re-conquered my kingdom. The trip so far hasn't really been any different from other similar journeys made in previous years.

All that remains now is Russia. And then what will I do? Continue making commitments in order to keep moving or stop and see what the results have been?

I still haven't reached a decision. I only know that a life without cause is a life without effect. And I can't allow that to happen to me. If necessary, I'll spend the rest of the year travelling.

I'm in the African city of Tunis, in Tunisia. The talk is about to begin and – thank heavens – the room is packed. I'm going to be introduced by two local intellectuals. In the short meeting we held beforehand, one of them showed me a text that would take just two minutes to deliver and the other a veritable thesis on my work that would take at least half an hour.

The coordinator very tactfully explains to the latter that since the event is only supposed to last, at most, fifty minutes, there won't be time for him to read his piece. I imagine how hard he must have worked on that essay, but the coordinator is right. The purpose of my visit to Tunis is to meet my readers. There is a brief discussion, after which the author of the essay says that he no longer wishes to take part and he leaves.

The talk begins. The introductions and acknowledgements take only five minutes; the rest of the time is free for open dialogue. I tell the audience that I haven't come here to explain anything, and that, ideally, the event should be more of a conversation than a presentation.

A young woman asks about the signs I speak of in my books. What form do they take? I explain that signs are an extremely personal language that we develop throughout our lives, by trial and error, until we begin to understand that God is guiding us. Someone else asks if a sign had brought me all the way to Tunisia. Without going into any detail, I say that it had.

The conversation continues, time passes quickly and I need to wrap things up. For the last question, I choose, at random, out of the six hundred people there, a middle-aged man with a bushy moustache.

Aleph

'I don't want to ask a question,' he says. 'I just want to say a name.'

The name he pronounces is that of Barbazan-Debat, a chapel in the middle of nowhere, thousands of kilometres from here, the same chapel where, one day, I placed a plaque in gratitude for a miracle and which I had visited, before setting out on this pilgrimage, in order to pray for Our Lady's protection.

I don't know how to respond. The following words were written by one of the other people on stage with me.

In the room, the Universe seemed suddenly to have stopped moving. So many things happened: I saw your tears and the tears of your dear wife, when that anonymous reader pronounced the name of that distant chapel.

You could no longer speak. Your smiling face grew serious. Your eyes filled with shy tears that trembled on your lashes, as if wishing to apologise for appearing there uninvited.

Even I had a lump in my throat, although I didn't know why. I looked for my wife and daughter in the audience, because I always look to them whenever I feel myself to be on the brink of something unknown. They were there, but they were sitting as silently as everyone else, their eyes fixed on you, trying to support you with their gaze, as if a gaze could ever support anyone.

Then I looked to Christina for help, trying to understand what was going on, how to bring to an end that seemingly interminable silence. And I saw that she was silently crying too, as if you were both notes from the same symphony and as if your tears were touching, even though you were sitting far apart.

For several long seconds, nothing existed, there was no room, no audience, nothing. You and your wife had set off for a place where we could not follow; all that remained was the joy of living, expressed in silence and emotion.

Words are tears that have been written down. Tears are words that need to be shed. Without them, joy loses all its brilliance and sadness has no end. Thank you, then, for your tears.

I should have said to the young woman who asked the first question about signs that *this* was a sign, confirming that I was where I should be, in the right place, at the right time, even though I didn't understand what had brought me there.

I suspect there was no need though. She would probably have understood anyway.*

---

* Author's note: Immediately after the talk, I sought out the man with the moustache. His name was Christian Dhellemmes. Afterwards, we exchanged a few emails, but never met again face to face. He died on 19 July 2009, in Tarbes, France.

36

Aleph

My wife and I are walking along, hand-in-hand, through the bazaar in Tunis, 15 kilometres from the ruins of Carthage, which, centuries before, had defied the might of Rome. We are discussing the great Carthaginian warrior, Hannibal. Since Carthage and Rome were separated by only a few hundred kilometres of sea, the Romans were expecting a sea battle. Instead, Hannibal took his vast army and crossed first the desert and then the Straits of Gibraltar, marched through Spain and France, climbed the Alps with soldiers and elephants, and attacked the Romans from the north, scoring one of the most resounding military victories ever recorded.

He overcame all the enemies in his path and yet – for reasons we still do not understand – he stopped short of conquering Rome and failed to attack at the right moment. As a result of his indecision, Carthage was wiped from the map by the Roman legions.

'Hannibal stopped and was defeated,' I say, thinking out loud. 'I'm glad that I'm able to go on, even though the beginning was difficult. I'm starting to get used to the journey now.'

My wife pretends not to have heard, because she realises that I'm trying to convince myself of something. We're on our way to a café to meet one of my readers, Samil, chosen at random at the post-talk party. I ask him to avoid all the usual monuments and tourist sights and show us where the real life of the city goes on.

He takes us to a beautiful building where, in 1754, a man killed his own brother. The brothers' father resolved to build this palace as a school, as a way of keeping alive the memory of his murdered son. I say that surely the son who had committed the murder would also be remembered.

'It's not quite like that,' says Samil. 'In our culture, the criminal shares his guilt with everyone who allowed him to commit the crime. When a man is murdered, the person who sold him the weapon is also responsible before God. The only way in which the father could correct what he perceived as his own mistake was to transform the tragedy into something useful to others.'

Suddenly everything vanishes – the palace, the street, the city, Africa. I take a gigantic leap into the dark and enter a tunnel that emerges into a damp dungeon. I'm standing before J. in one of my many previous lives, two hundred years before the crime committed in that house. He fixes me with stern, admonitory eyes.

I return just as quickly to the present. It all happened in a fraction of a second. I'm back at the palace, with Samil, my wife and the hubbub of the street in Tunis. But why that dip into the past? Why do the roots of the Chinese bamboo insist on poisoning the plant? That life was lived and the price paid.

'You were cowardly only once, while I acted unfairly many times. But that discovery freed me,' J. had said in Saint Martin, he, who had never encouraged me to go back into the past, who was vehemently opposed to the books, manuals and exercises that taught such things.

'Instead of resorting to vengeance, which would be merely a one-off punishment, he created a school in which wisdom and learning was passed on for more than two centuries,' Samil says.

I haven't missed a single word he has said and yet I also made that gigantic leap back in time.

'That's it.'

'What is?' asks my wife.

'I'm walking. I'm beginning to understand. It's all making sense.'

I feel euphoric. Samil is confused.

'What does Islam have to say about reincarnation?' I ask.

Samil looks at me, surprised.

'I've no idea, I'm not a scholar,' he says.

I ask him to find out. He takes his mobile phone and starts ringing various people. Christina and I go to a bar and order two strong black coffees. We're both tired, but we'll be having a seafood supper later on and have to resist the temptation to have a snack now.

'I just had a déjà vu moment,' I tell her.

'Everyone has them from time to time. You don't have to be a magus to have one,' jokes Christina.

Of course not, but déjà vu is more than just that fleeting moment of surprise, instantly forgotten because we never bother with things that make no sense.

It shows that time doesn't pass. It's a leap into something we have already experienced and that is being repeated.

Samil has vanished.

'While he was telling us about the palace, I was drawn back into the past for a millisecond. I'm sure this happened when he was talking about how any crime was not only the responsibility of the murderer, but of all those who created the conditions in which the crime could occur. The first time I met J., in 1982, he talked about my connection with his father. He never mentioned the subject again, and I forgot about it too. But a few moments ago, I saw his father. And I understand now what he meant.'

'In the life you told me about …?'

'Yes, during the Spanish Inquisition.'

'That's all over. Why torment yourself over something that's ancient history now?'

'I'm not tormenting myself. I learned long ago that in order to heal my wounds, I must have the courage to face up to them. I also learned to forgive myself and correct my mistakes. However, ever since I started out on this journey, I've had a sense of being confronted by a vast jigsaw puzzle, the pieces of which are only just beginning to be revealed, pieces of love, hate, sacrifice, forgiveness, joy and grief. That's why I'm here with you. I feel much better now, as if I really were going in search of my soul, of my kingdom, rather than sitting around complaining that I can't assimilate everything I've learned. I can't do that because I don't understand it all properly, but when I do, the truth will set me free.'

Samil is back, carrying a book. He sits down with us, consults his notes and respectfully turns the pages of the book, murmuring words in Arabic.

'I spoke to three scholars,' he says at last. 'Two of them said that, after death, the just go to Paradise. The third one, though, told me to consult some verses from the Koran.'

I can see that he's excited.

'Here's the first one, 2:28: *"Allah will cause you to die, and then he will bring you back to life again, and you will return to Him once more."* My translation isn't perfect, but that's what it means.'

He leafs feverishly through the sacred book. He translates the second verse, 2:154:

'*"Do not say of those who died in the name of Allah: They are dead. For they are alive, even though you cannot see them."*'

'Exactly!'

'There are other verses, but, to be honest, I don't feel very comfortable talking about this right now. I'd rather tell you about Tunis.'

'You've told us quite enough. People never leave, we are always here in our past and future lives. It appears in the Bible too, you know. I remember a passage in which Jesus refers to John the Baptist as the incarnation of Elias: "And if you will receive it, he [John] is the Elias who was to come." And there are other verses on the same subject,' I say.

He starts telling us some of the legends that surround the founding of the city, and I understand that it's time to get up and continue our walk.

Above one of the gates in the ancient city wall is a lantern, and Samil explains its significance to us:

'This is the origin of one of the most famous Arabic proverbs: "The light falls only on the stranger".'

The proverb, he says, is very apt for the situation we're in now. Samil wants to be a writer and is fighting to gain recognition in his own country, whereas I, a Brazilian author, am already known here.

I tell him that we have a similar saying: 'No one is a prophet in his own land.' We always tend to value what comes from afar, never recognising the beauty around us.

'Although sometimes,' I go on, 'we need to be strangers to ourselves. Then the hidden light in our soul will illuminate what we need to see.'

My wife appears not to be following the conversation, but at one point, she turns to me and says:

'There's something about that lantern, I can't quite explain what it is, but it's something to do with your situation now. As soon as I work out what it is, I'll tell you.'

We sleep for a while, have supper with friends and go for another walk round the city. Only then does my wife manage to explain what she had felt during the afternoon:

'You're travelling, but, at the same time, you haven't left home. As long as we're together, that will continue to be the case, because you have someone by your side who knows you, and this gives you a false sense of familiarity. It's time you continued on alone. You may find solitude oppressive, too much to bear, but that feeling will gradually disappear as you come more into contact with other people.'

After a pause, she adds:

'I once read that in a forest of a hundred thousand trees, no two leaves are alike. And no two journeys along the same Path are alike. If we continue to travel together, trying to make things fit our world-view, neither of us will benefit. So I give you my blessing and say: I'll see you in Germany for the first match in the World Cup!'

If a Cold Wind Blows

When I arrive at the Moscow hotel with my publisher and my editor, a young woman is waiting outside for me. She comes over and grasps my hands in hers.

'I need to talk to you. I've come all the way from Ekaterinburg to do just that.'

I'm tired. I woke up earlier than usual and had to change planes in Paris because there was no direct flight. I tried to sleep on the journey, but every time I managed to drop off, I would fall into the same unpleasant, recurring dream.

My publisher tells her that there will be a signing session tomorrow and that, in three days' time, we'll be in Ekaterinburg, the first stop on my train journey. I hold out my hand to say goodbye and notice that hers is very cold.

'Why didn't you wait for me inside?'

What I would really like to ask is how she found out which hotel I'm staying at, but that probably wouldn't be so very hard, and it isn't the first time this kind of thing has happened.

'I read your blog the other day and realised that you were talking directly to me.'

Aleph

I was beginning to post my thoughts about the journey on a blog. It was still in the experimental stage, and since I wrote the pieces ahead of time, I didn't know which article she was referring to. Even so, there could certainly have been no reference in it to her, given that I had only met her a few seconds before.

She takes out a piece of paper containing the article. I know it by heart, although I can't remember who told me the story. A man called Ali is in need of money and asks his boss to help him out. His boss sets him a challenge: if he can spend all night on the top of a mountain, he will receive a great reward; if he fails, he will have to work for free. The story continues:

When he left the shop, Ali noticed that an icy wind was blowing. He felt afraid and decided to ask his best friend, Aydi, if he thought he was mad to accept the wager. After considering the matter for a moment, Aydi answered, 'Don't worry, I'll help you. Tomorrow night, when you're sitting on top of the mountain, look straight ahead. I'll be on the top of the mountain opposite, where I'll keep a fire burning all night for you. Look at the fire and think of our friendship; and that will keep you warm. You'll make it through the night, and afterwards, I'll ask you for something in return.'

Ali won the wager, got the money, and went to his friend's house.

'You said you wanted some sort of payment in return.'

Aydi said, 'Yes, but it isn't money. Promise that if ever a cold wind blows through my life, you will light the fire of friendship for me.'

I thank the young woman for her kindness and tell her that I'm very busy, but that if she wants to go to the one signing session I'll be giving in Moscow, I'll be happy to sign one of her books.

'That isn't why I came. I know about your journey across Russia by train, and I'm going with you. When I read your first book, I heard a voice saying that you once lit a sacred fire for me and that one day I would have to repay the favour. I dreamed about that fire night after night and even thought I would have to go to Brazil to find you. I know you need help, which is why I'm here.'

The people with me laugh. I try to be polite, saying that I'm sure we'll see each other the next day. My publisher explains to her that someone is waiting for me, and I seize on that as an excuse to say goodbye.

'My name is Hilal,' she says before she leaves.

Ten minutes later, I'm in my hotel room and have already forgotten about the girl who approached me outside the hotel. I can't even remember her name, and if I were to meet her again now, I wouldn't recognise her. However, something has left me feeling vaguely uneasy: in her eyes I saw both love and death.

take off all my clothes, turn on the shower and stand beneath the water – one of my favourite rituals.

I position my head so that all I can hear is the sound of the water in my ears, which cuts me off from everything else, transporting me into a different world. Like a conductor aware of every instrument in the orchestra, I begin to distinguish every sound, each one of which becomes a word. I can't understand those words, but I know they exist.

The tiredness, anxiety and feeling of disorientation that come from visiting so many different countries vanish. With each day that passes, I can see that the long journey is having the desired effect. J. was right. I had been allowing myself to be slowly poisoned by routine: showers were merely a matter of washing my skin clean, meals were for feeding my body, and the sole purpose of walks was to avoid heart problems in the future.

Now things are changing, imperceptibly, but they are changing. Meals are times when I can venerate the presence and the teachings of friends; walks are once again meditations on the present moment; and the sound of water in my ears silences my thoughts, calms me and makes me relearn that it is these small daily gestures that bring us closer to God, as long as I am able to give each gesture the value it deserves.

When J. said to me, 'Leave your comfortable life and go in search of your kingdom,' I felt betrayed, confused, abandoned. I was hoping for a solution or an answer to my doubts, something that would console me and help me feel at peace with my soul again. Those who set off in search of their kingdom know that they are going to find, instead, only challenges, long periods of waiting, unexpected changes, or, even worse, nothing.

I'm exaggerating. If we seek something, that same thing is seeking us.

Nevertheless, you have to be prepared for everything. At this point, I make the decision I've been needing to make: even if I find nothing on this train journey, I will carry on, because I've known since that moment of realisation in the hotel in London that, although my roots are ready, my soul has been slowly dying from something very hard to detect and even harder to cure.

Routine.

Routine has nothing to do with repetition. To become really good at anything, you have to practise and repeat, practise and repeat, until the technique becomes intuitive. I learned this when I was a child, in a small town in the interior of Brazil, where my family used to spend the summer holidays. I was fascinated by the work of a blacksmith who lived nearby. I would sit, for what seemed like an eternity, watching his hammer rise and fall on the red-hot steel, scattering sparks all around, like fireworks. Once he said to me:

'You probably think I'm doing the same thing over and over, don't you?'

'Yes,' I said.

'Well, you're wrong. Each time I bring the hammer down, the intensity of the blow is different. Sometimes it's harder, sometimes it's softer. But I only learned that after I'd been repeating the same gesture for many years, until the moment came when I didn't have to think, I simply let my hand guide my work.'

I've never forgotten those words.

Sharing Souls

I look at each of my readers. I hold out my hand and thank them for being there. My body may be travelling, but when my soul flies from city to city, I am never alone: I am all the many people I meet and who have understood my soul through my books. I'm not a stranger here in Moscow, or in London, Sofia, Tunis, Kiev, Santiago de Compostela, Guimarães or any of the other cities I've visited in the last month and a half.

I can hear an argument going on behind me, but I try to concentrate on what I'm doing. The argument, however, shows no sign of abating. Finally, I turn round and ask my publisher what the problem is.

'It's that girl from yesterday. She says she wants to be near you.'

I can't even recall the girl from yesterday, but I ask them at least to stop arguing. I carry on signing books.

Someone sits down close to me only to be removed by one of the uniformed security guards, and the argument starts again. I stop what I'm doing.

Beside me is the girl whose eyes speak of love and death. For the first time, I take a proper look at her: dark

hair, between twenty-two and twenty-nine years old
(I'm useless at judging people's ages), a beat-up leather
jacket, jeans and trainers.

'We've checked the backpack,' says the security man,
'and there's nothing to worry about. But she can't stay
here.'

The girl simply smiles. A reader is waiting for this
conversation to end so that I can sign his books. I realise
that the girl is not going to leave.

'My name's Hilal, don't you remember? I came to light
the sacred fire.'

I lie and say that yes, of course I remember. The
people in the queue are beginning to grow impatient.
The reader at the head of the queue says something in
Russian to her, and judging from his tone of voice, I
sense that it was nothing very pleasant.

There is a proverb in Portuguese which says: 'What
can't be cured must be endured.' Since I don't have time
for arguments now and need to make a quick decision,
I simply ask her to move slightly further off, so that I can
have a little privacy with the people waiting. She does
as asked, and goes and stands at a discreet distance from
me.

Seconds later, I have once again forgotten her existence and I'm concentrating on the task in hand.
Everyone thanks me and I thank them in return, and the
four hours pass as if I were in paradise. I take a cigarette-
break every hour, but I'm not in the least tired. I leave

each book-signing session with my batteries recharged and with more energy than ever.

Afterwards, I call for a round of applause for the organisers. It's time to move on to my next engagement. The girl whose existence I had forgotten comes over to me.

'I have something important to show you,' she says.

'That's not going to be possible,' I say. 'I have a supper to go to.'

'It's perfectly possible,' she replies. 'My name is Hilal. I was waiting for you yesterday outside your hotel. And I can show you what I want to show you here and now, while you're waiting to leave.'

Before I can respond, she takes a violin out of her backpack and starts to play.

The readers, who had begun to drift away, return for this impromptu concert. Hilal plays with her eyes closed, as if she were in a trance. I watch the bow moving back and forth, lightly touching the strings and producing this music, which, even though I've never heard it before, is saying something that I and everyone else present need to hear. Sometimes she pauses; sometimes she seems to be in a state of ecstasy; sometimes her whole being dances with the instrument; but mostly only her upper body and her hands move.

Every note leaves in each of us a memory, but it is the melody as a whole that tells a story, the story of someone wanting to get closer to another person and who keeps on trying despite repeated rejections. While Hilal is playing, I remember the many occasions on which help has come from precisely those people whom I thought had nothing to add to my life.

When she stops playing, there is no applause, nothing, only an almost palpable silence.

'Thank you,' I say.

'I've shared a little of my soul, but there is still a lot to do before I can fulfil my mission. May I come with you?'

Generally speaking, pushy people provoke one of two reactions in me: either I turn and walk away or I allow myself to be beguiled. I can't tell someone that their dreams are impossible. Not everyone has the strength of mind that Mônica showed in that bar in Catalonia, and if I were to persuade just one person to stop fighting for something they were convinced was worthwhile, I would end up persuading myself, and my whole life would be diminished.

It has been a very satisfying day. I phone the Brazilian ambassador and ask if he could include another guest at supper. Very kindly, he agrees, saying that my readers are my representatives.

Despite the formal atmosphere, the ambassador manages to put everyone at their ease. Hilal arrives wearing an outfit that I consider to be tasteless in the extreme, full of gaudy colours, in sharp contrast with the sober dress of the other guests. Not knowing quite where to put this last-minute arrival, the organisers end up seating her in the place of honour, next to our host.

Before we sit down to supper, my best friend in Russia, an industrialist, explains that we're going to have problems with the sub-agent, who spent the whole of the cocktail party prior to supper arguing with her husband over the phone.

'About what exactly?'

'It seems that you agreed to go to the club where he's the manager, but cancelled at the last minute.'

There *was* something in my diary along the lines of 'discuss the menu for the journey through Siberia', which was the least and most irrelevant of my concerns on an afternoon during which I had received only positive energy. I cancelled the meeting because it seemed so absurd; I've never discussed menus in my entire life. I preferred to go back to the hotel, take a shower and let the sound of the water carry me off to places I can't even explain to myself.

Supper is served, parallel conversations spring up around the table and, at one point, the ambassador's wife kindly asks Hilal about herself.

'I was born in Turkey and came to study violin in Ekaterinburg when I was twelve. I assume you know how musicians are selected?'

No, the ambassador's wife doesn't. Suddenly, there seem to be fewer parallel conversations going on.

Perhaps everyone is interested in that awkward young woman in the garish clothes.

'Any child who starts playing an instrument has to practise for a set number of hours per week. At that stage, they're all deemed capable of performing in an orchestra one day. As they grow older, some start practising more than others. In the end, there is just a small group of outstanding students, who practise for nearly forty hours a week. Scouts from big orchestras visit the music schools in search of new talent, who are then invited to turn professional. That's what happened to me.'

'It would seem that you found your vocation,' says the ambassador. 'We're not all so lucky.'

'It wasn't exactly my vocation. I started practising a lot because I was sexually abused when I was ten.'

All conversation around the table stops. The ambassador tries to change the subject and makes some comment about Brazil negotiating with Russia on the export and import of heavy machinery, but no one, absolutely no one, is interested in my country's trade balance. It falls to me to pick up the thread of the story.

'Hilal, if you wouldn't mind, I think everyone here would be interested to know what relation there is between being a young sex abuse victim and becoming a violin virtuoso.'

'What does your name mean?' asks the ambassador's wife, in a last desperate attempt to take the conversation off in another direction.

'In Turkish it means new moon. It's the symbol on our national flag. My father was an ardent nationalist. Actually, it's a name more common among boys than girls. It has another meaning in Arabic apparently, but I don't quite know what.'

I refuse to be sidetracked.

'To go back to what we were talking about, would you mind explaining? We're among family.'

Family?! Most of the people here met for the first time over supper.

Everyone seems suddenly very preoccupied with their plates, cutlery and glasses, pretending to be concentrating on the food, but longing to know the rest of her story. Hilal speaks as if what she was talking about were the most natural thing in the world.

'It was a neighbour, whom everyone thought of as gentle and helpful, a good man to have around in an emergency. He was married and had two daughters my age. Whenever I went to his house to play with them, he would sit me on his knee and tell me nice stories. While he was doing this, however, his hand would be wandering all over my body, and at first I took this as a sign of affection. As time passed, though, he began touching me between my legs and asking me to touch his penis, things like that.'

She looks at the other five women around the table and says:

'It's not at all uncommon, unfortunately. Wouldn't you agree?'

No one answers, but my instinct tells me that at least one or two would have experienced something similar.

'Anyway, that wasn't the only problem. The worst thing was that I started to enjoy it, even though I knew it was wrong. Then, one day, I decided not to go back there, despite my parents telling me that I ought to play with our neighbour's daughters more. At the time I was learning the violin and so I told them that I wasn't getting on well in my classes and needed to practise more. I started playing compulsively, desperately.'

No one moves. No one knows quite what to say.

'And because I carried all that guilt around inside me, because victims always end up considering themselves to be the culprits, I decided to keep punishing myself. So, in my relationships with men, I've always sought suffering, conflict and despair.'

She looks straight at me, and the whole table notices.

'But that's going to change now, isn't that right?'

Having been in charge of the situation up to that point, I suddenly lose control. All I can do is mutter 'Yes, well, I hope so' and quickly steer the conversation round to the beautiful building that houses the Brazilian embassy in Russia.

When we leave, I ask where Hilal is staying and check with my industrialist friend if he would mind taking her home before dropping me off at my hotel. He agrees.

'Thank you for the violin music, and thank you for sharing your story with a group of perfect strangers. Now, each morning, when your mind is still empty, devote a little time to the Divine. The air contains a cosmic force for which every culture has a different name, but that doesn't matter. The important thing is to do what I'm telling you now. Inhale deeply and ask for all the blessings in the air to enter your body and fill every cell. Then exhale slowly, projecting happiness and peace around you. Repeat this ten times. You'll be helping to heal yourself and contributing to healing the world as well.'

'What do you mean?'

'Nothing. Just do the exercise. You'll gradually eradicate your negative feelings about love. Don't let yourself be destroyed by a force that was placed in our hearts in order to make everything better. Breathe in, inhaling whatever exists in the heavens and on earth. Breathe out beauty and fecundity. Believe me, it will work.'

'I didn't come here to learn an exercise I could find in any book on yoga,' says Hilal angrily.

Outside, Moscow is parading past us. What I would really like is to wander the streets and have a coffee somewhere, but it's been a long day and I have to get up early tomorrow for a series of engagements.

'So I can come with you, then?'

Can she talk of nothing else? I met her less than 24 hours ago – if you can call such a strange encounter a meeting. My friend laughs. I try to remain serious.

58

'Look, I took you to the ambassador's supper. Isn't that enough? I'm not making this journey to promote my books,' I hesitate. 'I'm doing it for personal reasons.'

'Yes, I know.'

Something about the way she says this makes me feel that she really does know, but I choose not to trust my instincts.

'I've made many men suffer and I've suffered greatly too,' Hilal goes on. 'The light of love flows out of my soul, but it can go nowhere because it's blocked by pain. I could inhale and exhale every morning for the rest of my life, but that wouldn't solve anything. I've tried to express my love through the violin, but that's not enough either. I know that you can heal me and that I can heal what you're feeling. I've lit a fire on the mountain opposite yours, you can count on me.'

Why was she saying this?

'What hurts us is what heals us,' she said. 'Life has been very hard on me, but, at the same time, it has taught me a great deal. You can't see it, but my body is covered in open wounds that are constantly bleeding. I wake each morning wanting to die before the day is out, but I continue to live, suffering and fighting, fighting and suffering, clinging on to the certainty that it will all end one day. Please, don't leave me alone here. This journey is my salvation.'

My friend stops the car, puts his hand in his pocket and hands Hilal a wad of notes.

'He doesn't own the train,' he says. 'Take this; it should be more than enough for a second-class ticket and three meals a day.'

Then turning to me, he says:

'You know the pain I'm going through at the moment. The woman I love has died, and I, too, could inhale and exhale for the rest of my life, but I'm never going to be truly happy again. My wounds are open and bleeding too. I understand exactly what this young woman is saying. I know you're making this journey for entirely personal reasons, but don't leave her alone like this. If you believe in the words you write, allow the people around you to grow with you.'

'OK, fine,' I say to her. 'He's right, I don't own the train, but I just want you to know that I'm going to be surrounded by people most of the time, so there won't be many opportunities to talk.'

My friend starts the engine again and drives for another fifteen minutes in silence. We reach a leafy square. She tells him where to park, jumps out and says goodbye. I get out of the car and accompany her to the door of the house where she's staying with friends.

She kisses me briefly on the lips.

'Your friend is mistaken, but if I were to look too happy, he might take his money back,' she says, smiling. 'My suffering is nothing compared to his. Besides, I've never been as happy as I am now, because I followed the signs, I was patient, and I know that this is going to change everything.'

She turns and goes into the building.

Only then, as I walk back to the car, looking at my friend who has got out to smoke a cigarette and is smiling because he saw that quick kiss, only then, as I listen to the wind in the trees restored to life by the force of the Spring, am I aware that I'm in a city I don't know very well, but which I love, only then, as I feel for the pack of cigarettes in my pocket, thinking that tomorrow I'll be setting off on a long-dreamed-of adventure, only then …

… only then do I remember the warning given by the clairvoyant I met at Véronique's house. He'd said something about Turkey, but quite what I can't remember.

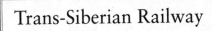

Trans-Siberian Railway

Note: The numbers in parentheses indicate the time difference between cities, taking Moscow as the reference point

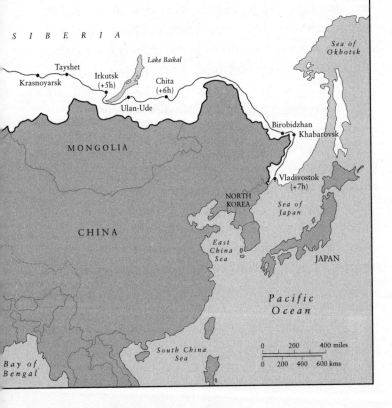

FEDERATION

SIBERIA

Lake Baikal

Tayshet

Krasnoyarsk

Irkutsk (+5h)

Chita (+6h)

Ulan-Ude

Sea of Okhotsk

Birobidzhan

Khabarovsk

MONGOLIA

Vladivostok (+7h)

NORTH KOREA

Sea of Japan

CHINA

East China Sea

JAPAN

Pacific Ocean

South China Sea

Bay of Bengal

0   200   400 miles

0   200   400   600 kms

9,288

The Trans-Siberian railway is one of the longest railways in the world. You can start your journey at any station in Europe, but the Russian section is 9,288 kilometres long, connecting hundreds of small and large cities, traversing 76 per cent of the country and passing through seven different time zones. When I enter the train station in Moscow, at eleven o'clock at night, day has already dawned in Vladivostok, our final destination.

Until the end of the nineteenth century, few travellers ventured into Siberia, which holds the record for the lowest temperature ever registered in a permanently inhabited place: –72.2°C in the town of Oymyakon. The rivers that linked the region to the rest of the world used to be the main means of transport, but they were frozen for eight months of the year. The population of Central Asia lived in almost complete isolation, although it was the source of most of the then Russian Empire's natural wealth. For strategic and political reasons, Alexander II approved the construction of the railway, the cost of which was exceeded only by Imperial

Russia's military budget during the whole of the First World War.

During the civil war that erupted immediately after the Communist Revolution of 1917, the railway became the focus of fighting. Forces loyal to the deposed emperor, notably the Czech Legion, used armoured carriages, which acted as tanks on rails, and were thus able to repel attacks by the Red Army with relative ease, as long as they were kept supplied with munitions and provisions from the East. That was when the saboteurs were sent into action, blowing up bridges and cutting communications. The pro-Imperial forces were driven to the outer reaches of the Russian continent and many crossed Alaska and into Canada, from where they dispersed to other countries.

When I entered the station at Moscow, the price of a ticket from Europe to the Pacific Ocean in a compartment shared with three other people could cost anything between 30 and 60 euros.

My first photo was of the departures board showing our train due to leave at 23.15! My heart was beating fast, as if I were a child again, watching my toy train chugging round the room and letting my mind travel to distant places, as distant as the one in which I found myself now.

My conversation with J. in Saint Martin just over three months before felt as if it had happened in a previous incarnation. What idiotic questions I had asked! What was the meaning of life? Why can I make no progress? Why is the spiritual world moving further and further away? The answer couldn't have been simpler: because I wasn't really living!

How good it was to go back to being a child, feeling my blood flowing in my veins and my eyes shining, thrilling to the sight of the crowded platform, the smell of oil and food, the squeal of brakes as a train came into the station, the shrill sounds of luggage vans and whistles.

To live is to experience things, not sit around pondering the meaning of life. Obviously, not everyone needs to cross Asia or follow the Road to Santiago. I knew an abbot in Austria, who rarely left his monastery in Melk, and yet he understood the world far better than many travellers I have met. I have a friend who experienced great spiritual revelations just from watching his children sleeping. When my wife starts work on a new painting, she enters a kind of trance and speaks to her guardian angel.

But I am a born pilgrim. Even when I'm feeling really lazy or I'm missing home, I need take only one step to be carried away by the excitement of the journey. In Yaroslavl station, making my way over to platform 5, I realise that I will never reach my goal by staying in the same place all the time. I can only speak to my soul when the two of us are off exploring deserts or cities or mountains or roads.

Aleph

We are in the last carriage, which will be coupled and decoupled at various stations along the way. I can't see the engine from where I am, only the giant steel snake of the train and various other passengers – Mongols, Tatars, Russians, Chinese – some sitting on huge trunks, and all waiting for the doors to open. People come over to talk to me, but I move away. I don't want to think about anything else, apart from the fact that I'm here, now, ready for yet another departure, a new challenge.

This moment of childish ecstasy must have lasted at most five minutes, but I took in every detail, every sound, every smell. I won't be able to remember anything afterwards, but that doesn't matter: time is not a cassette tape that can be wound and rewound.

Don't think about what you'll tell people afterwards. The time is here and now. Make the most of it.

I approach the rest of the group and realise that they're all as excited as I am. I'm introduced to the translator who will be travelling with me. His name is Yao. He was born in China, but went to Brazil as a refugee during the civil war in his country. He then studied in Japan and is now a retired language teacher from the University of Moscow. He must be about seventy. He is tall and the only one in the group who is impeccably dressed in suit and tie.

'My name means "very distant",' he says to break the ice.

'My name means "little rock",' I tell him, smiling. In fact I have had the same smile on my face since last night, when I could barely sleep for thinking about today's adventure. I couldn't be in a better mood.

The omnipresent Hilal is standing near the carriage I'll be travelling in, even though her compartment must be far from mine. I wasn't surprised to see her there. I assumed she would be. I blow her a kiss and she responds with a smile. At some point on the journey, I'm sure we'll enjoy an interesting conversation or two.

I stand very still, intent on every detail around me, like a navigator about to set sail in search of the *Mare Ignotum*. My translator respects my silence, but I realise that something is wrong, because my publisher seems preoccupied. I ask Yao what's going on.

He explains that the person representing me in Russia has not arrived. I remember the conversation with my friend the night before, but what does it matter? If she hasn't turned up, that's her problem.

I notice Hilal say something to my editor. She receives a brusque reply, but doesn't lose her cool, just as she didn't when I told her we couldn't meet. I am getting to like the fact that she is here more and more; I like her determination, her poise. The two women are arguing now.

I again ask the translator to explain what's going on, and he says that my editor has asked Hilal to go back to her own carriage. Fat chance, I think to myself; that young woman will do exactly what she wants. I amuse myself by observing the only things I can understand: intonation and body language. When I think the moment is right, I go over to them, still smiling.

'Come on, let's not start off on a negative vibe. We're all happy and excited, setting off on a journey none of us has ever made before.'

'But she wants—'

'Just leave her alone. She can go to her own compartment later on.'

My editor does not insist.

The doors open with a noise that echoes down the platform, and people start to move. Who are these people climbing into the carriages? What does this journey mean to each passenger? A reunion with their loved one, a family visit, a quest for wealth, a triumphant or shamefaced return home, a discovery, an adventure, a need to flee or to find? The train is filling up with all these possibilities.

Hilal picks up her luggage – which consists of her backpack and a brightly coloured bag – and prepares to climb into the carriage with us. The editor is smiling as if she were pleased with the way the argument had ended, but I know that she will seize the first opportunity to take her revenge. There's no point explaining that all we achieve by exacting revenge is to make ourselves the equals of our enemies, whereas by forgiving we show wisdom and intelligence. Apart from monks in the Himalayas and saints in the deserts, I think we all have these vengeful feelings, because they're an essential part of the human condition. We shouldn't judge ourselves too harshly.

Our carriage comprises four compartments, bathrooms, a small lounge area, where I assume we will spend most of the time, and a kitchen.

I go to my compartment, which consists of a double bed, wardrobe, a table and chair facing the window, and a door that opens onto one of the bathrooms. At the end is another door. I go over and open it and see that it leads into an empty room. It would seem that the two compartments share the same bathroom.

Ah, it was obviously intended for the representative who did not turn up. But what does that matter?

The whistle sounds. The train slowly starts to move. We all rush to the lounge window and wave goodbye to people we've never seen before. We watch the platform rapidly being left behind, the lights passing faster and faster, the tracks, the dim electric cables. I'm impressed by how quiet everyone is; none of us wants to talk, we are all dreaming about what might happen, and no one,

I'm sure, is thinking about what they've left behind, rather about what lies ahead.

When the tracks disappear into the black night, we sit around the table. There's a basket of fruit we could eat, but we had supper in Moscow, and the only thing that awakens everyone's interest is a gleaming bottle of vodka, which we immediately open. We drink and talk about everything but the journey, because that is the present, not the past. We drink some more and begin to reveal what we all expect from the coming days. We continue to drink, and an infectious joy fills the room. Suddenly it's as if we've known each other all our lives.

The translator tells me something of his life and passions: literature, travelling and the martial arts. As it happens, I learned aikido when I was young, and he says that if we get bored at any point and run out of conversation, we can always do a little training in the tiny corridor beside the compartments.

Hilal is talking to the editor who hadn't wanted her to get into the carriage. I know that both are trying to patch up their misunderstanding, but I know, too, that tomorrow is another day, and confinement together in a small space tends to exacerbate conflicts, and another argument is sure to break out. Not for a while though, I hope.

The translator appears to have read my thoughts. He pours everyone more vodka and talks about how conflicts are resolved in aikido.

'It's not really fighting. What we aim to do is calm the spirit and get in touch with the source from which everything comes, removing any trace of malice or egotism. If you spend too much time trying to find out what is good or bad about someone else, you'll forget your own soul and end up exhausted and defeated by the energy you have wasted in judging others.'

No one seems very interested in what a man of seventy has to say. The initial euphoria provoked by the vodka gives way to a collective weariness. At one point, I get up to go to the toilet, and when I return, the room is empty.

Apart from Hilal, of course.

'Where is everyone?' I ask.

'They were being polite and waiting for you to leave, so that they could go to bed.'

'You'd better do the same.'

'But there's an empty compartment here—'

I pick up her backpack and bag, take her gently by the arm and lead her to the end of the carriage.

'Don't push your luck. Good night.'

She looks at me, but says nothing and heads for her compartment, although I have no idea where that is.

I retire to my room and my excitement becomes intense weariness. I place my computer on the table and my saints – who go everywhere with me – beside the bed, then I go to the bathroom to clean my teeth. This turns out to be a far harder task than I imagined. The glass of mineral water in my hand keeps lurching about with the movement of the train. After various attempts, I achieve my objective.

I put on the T-shirt I wear in bed, smoke a cigarette, turn out the light, close my eyes and imagine that the swaying is rather like being inside the womb and that I will spend a night blessed by the angels. A vain hope.

Hilal's Eyes

When day finally dawns, I get up, change my clothes and go into the lounge. Everyone else is there too, including Hilal.

'You have to write a note giving me permission to come back here,' she announces, before she has even said 'Good morning'. 'I had a terrible time getting here today, and the guards in every carriage said that they would only let me through if—'

I ignore her last words and greet the others. I ask if they had a good night.

'No,' comes the collective response.

So it wasn't just me.

'I slept really well,' says Hilal, unaware that she is provoking the general wrath of her fellow travellers. 'My carriage is right in the middle of the train and so it doesn't lurch about so much. This is the worst possible carriage to be travelling in.'

My publisher seems about to make some rude comment, but restrains himself. His wife looks out of the window and lights a cigarette to disguise her irritation. My editor pulls a face that says more clearly than any words: 'Didn't I tell you she'd be in the way?'

'Every day I'm going to write down a thought and stick it on the mirror,' says Yao, who also appears to have slept well.

He gets up, goes over to the mirror in the lounge and sticks a bit of paper on it, which says: 'If you want to see a rainbow you have to learn to like the rain.'

No one is too keen on this optimistic saying. One doesn't have to be a mind-reader to know what's going through everyone's head: 'Good grief, is this what it's going to be like for another nine thousand kilometres?'

'I've got a photo on my mobile phone I'd like to show you,' says Hilal. 'And I brought my violin with me, too, if anyone wants to listen to some music.'

We're already listening to the music from the radio in the kitchen. The tension in the carriage is rising. Any moment now, someone is going to explode, and I won't be able to do anything about it.

'Look, just let us eat our breakfast in peace. You're welcome to join us if you want. Then I'm going to try to get some sleep. I'll look at your photo later.'

There is a noise like thunder. A train passes, travelling in the opposite direction, something that happened throughout the night with frightening regularity. And far from reminding me of the gentle rocking of a cradle, the swaying of the carriage was much more like being inside a cocktail shaker. I feel physically ill and very guilty for having dragged all these other people along on my adventure. I'm beginning to understand why, in Portuguese, a fairground roller-coaster is called a *montanha-russa* or Russian mountain.

Hilal and Yao the translator make several attempts to start a conversation, but no one at the table – the publisher and his wife, the editor, the writer whose idea this trip was – takes them up. We eat our breakfast in silence. Outside, the landscape repeats itself over and over – small towns, forests, small towns, forests.

One of the publishers asks Yao: 'How long before we reach Ekaterinburg?'

'Just after midnight.'

There is a general sigh of relief. Perhaps we can change our minds and say that enough is enough. You don't need to climb a mountain in order to know that it's high; you don't have to go all the way to Vladivostok to be able to say that you've travelled on the Trans-Siberian railway.

'Right, I'm going to try and get some sleep.'

I stand up. Hilal stands up too.

'What about the piece of paper? And the photo on my mobile phone?'

Piece of paper? Ah, of course, the permission she needs to be able to visit our carriage. Before I can say anything, Yao has written something in Russian for me to sign. Everyone – including me – glares at him.

'Would you mind adding "once a day", please?'

76

Yao does this, then gets up and says that he'll go in search of a guard willing to stamp the document.

'And what about the photo?'

By now, I'll agree to anything if I can just return to my compartment and sleep, but I don't want to annoy my companions who are, after all, paying for this trip. I ask Hilal to go with me to the other end of the carriage. We open the first door and find ourselves in a small area with two exterior doors and a third leading to the next carriage. The noise there is unbearable because, as well as the racket made by the wheels on the rails, there is the grinding noise made by the metal plates linking the carriages.

Hilal shows me the photo on her mobile phone, possibly taken just after dawn. It's a photo of a long cloud in the sky.

'Do you see?'

Yes, I can see a cloud.

'We're being accompanied on this journey.'

We're being accompanied by a cloud that will long since have disappeared for ever. I continue to acquiesce, in the hope that the conversation will soon be over.

'Yes, you're right. But let's talk about it later. Now go back to your own compartment.'

'I can't. You only gave me permission to come here once a day.'

Tiredness must be affecting my reasoning powers, because I realise now that I have created a monster. If she can only come once a day, she'll arrive in the morning and not leave until night-time, an error I'll try to correct later.

'Listen, I'm a guest on this journey too. I'd love to have your company all the time, because you're always so full of energy and never take "No" for an answer, but you see ...'

Those eyes. Green and without a trace of make-up.

'... you see ...'

Perhaps I'm just exhausted. After more than twenty-four hours without sleep, we lose almost all our defences. That's the state I'm in now. The vestibule area, bare of any furniture, made only of glass and steel, is beginning to grow fuzzy. The noise is starting to diminish, my concentration is going, and I'm not entirely sure who or where I am. I know that I'm asking her to cooperate, to go back where she came from, but the words coming out of my mouth bear no relation to what I'm seeing.

I'm looking at the light, at a sacred place, and a wave washes over me, filling me with peace and love, two things that rarely come together. I can see myself, but, at the same time, I can see elephants in Africa waving their trunks, camels in the desert, people chatting in a bar in Buenos Aires, a dog crossing the street, the brush being wielded by a woman finishing a painting of a rose, snow melting on a mountain in Switzerland, monks singing exotic hymns, a pilgrim arriving at the cathedral in Santiago de Compostela, a shepherd with his sheep, soldiers who have just woken up and are preparing for war, the fish in the ocean, the cities and forests of the world – and everything is simultaneously very clear and very large, very small and very quiet.

I am in the Aleph, the point at which everything is in the same place at the same time.

I'm at a window looking out at the world and its secret places, poetry lost in time and words left hanging in space. Those eyes are telling me about things that we do not even know exist, but which are there, ready to be discovered and known only by souls, not by bodies. Sentences that are perfectly understood, even when left unspoken. Feelings that simultaneously exalt and suffocate.

I am standing before doors that open for a fraction of a second and then close again, but that give me a glimpse of what is hidden behind them – the treasures and traps, the roads never taken and the journeys never imagined.

'Why are you looking at me like that? Why are your eyes showing me all this?'

I'm not the one saying this, but the girl or woman standing before me. Our eyes have become the mirrors of our souls, mirrors not only of our souls perhaps, but of all the souls of all the people on this planet who are at this moment walking, loving, being born and dying, suffering or dreaming.

'It's not me … it's just …'

I cannot finish the sentence, because the doors continue to open and reveal their secrets. I see lies and truths, strange dances performed before what appears to be the image of a goddess, sailors battling the fierce sea, a couple sitting on a beach looking at the same sea, which looks calm and welcoming. The doors continue to open, the doors of Hilal's eyes, and I begin to see myself, as if we had known each other for a long, long time …

'What are you doing?' she asks.

'The Aleph …'

The tears of that girl or woman standing before me seem to want to leave by those same doors. Someone once said that tears are the blood of the soul, and that is what I'm beginning to see now, because I have entered a tunnel, I'm going back into the past, and she is waiting for me there too, her hands pressed together as if saying the most sacred prayer God ever gave to mankind. Yes, she is there before me, kneeling on the ground and smiling, telling me that love can save everything, but I look at my clothes, at my hands, in one of which I am holding a quill pen …

'Stop!' I shout.

Hilal closes her eyes.

I am once more in a train travelling to Siberia and beyond, to the Pacific Ocean. I feel even wearier than I did before, and although I understand exactly what has happened, I am incapable of explaining it.

Aleph

She embraces me. I embrace her and gently stroke her hair.

'I knew it,' she says. 'I knew I had met you before. I knew it the first time I saw your photograph. It's as if we had to meet again at some point in this life. I talked to my friends about it, but they thought I was crazy, that thousands of people must say the same thing about thousands of other people every day. I thought they must be right, but life … life brought you to me. You came to find me, didn't you?'

I am gradually recovering from what I have just experienced. I know what she's talking about, because, centuries before, I went through one of the doors I have just seen in her eyes. She was there, along with other people. Cautiously, I ask her what she saw.

'Everything. I don't think I will ever be able to explain this, but the moment I closed my eyes, I was in a safe, comfortable place, as if I were in my own house.'

No, she doesn't know what she's saying. She doesn't know yet. But I do. I pick up her bags and lead her back into the lounge.

'I haven't got the energy to think or speak right now. Sit over there, read something, let me rest a little and then I'll be right back. If anyone says anything, tell them that I asked you to stay.'

She does as asked. I go to my compartment, collapse onto the bed fully clothed and fall into a deep sleep.

*S*omeone knocks at the door.

'We'll be arriving in ten minutes.'

I open my eyes. It's night outside, or, rather, it's the early hours of the morning. I've slept all day and will have difficulties now getting back to sleep.

'They're going to uncouple the carriage and leave it in a siding, so take what you need for two nights in the city,' says the voice.

I open the shutters. Lights begin to appear, the train is slowing, we really are arriving. I wash my face and quickly pack whatever I will need for two nights in Ekaterinburg. What I experienced earlier is gradually beginning to come back to me.

When I leave the compartment, everyone is standing in the corridor, apart from Hilal, who is still sitting in the place where I left her. She doesn't smile, but simply shows me a piece of paper.

'Yao got me the permit.'

Yao looks at me and whispers:

'Have you ever read the *Tao Te Ching*?'

Yes, of course I have, like almost everyone of my generation.

'Then you'll remember these words: "Expend your energies and you will remain young."'

He nods slightly in the direction of the girl, who is still seated. I find this remark in bad taste.

'If you're insinuating—'

'I'm not insinuating anything. If you have misunderstood me, it's because that idea must be inside your head. What I meant, since you don't understand Lao Tzu's words, was: place all your feelings outside yourself and you will be renewed. As I understand it, she is the right person to help you.'

Have the two of them been talking? Was Yao passing by when we entered the Aleph? Did he see what was happening?

'Do you believe in a spiritual world, in a parallel universe, where time and space are eternal and always present?' I ask.

The brakes begin to squeal. Yao nods, but I can see that he is weighing his words. At last, he says:

'I don't believe in God as you imagine Him to be, but I believe in many things that you could never even dream of. If you're free tomorrow night, perhaps we could go for a walk together.'

The train stops. Hilal gets up and comes to join us. Yao smiles and embraces her. We all put on our coats and, at 1.04 in the morning, we step out into Ekaterinburg.

The Ipatiev House

The omnipresent Hilal has disappeared.

I come down from my room, assuming that I'll find her in the hotel lobby, but she isn't there. Despite spending most of yesterday flat out on my bed, I had still managed to sleep well once back on 'terra firma'. I phone Yao's room and we go out for a walk around the city. This is exactly what I need to do right now: to walk, walk, walk, breathe some fresh air, and take a look at a city I've never visited before and enjoy feeling that it's mine.

Yao tells me a few historical facts – Ekaterinburg is Russia's third largest city, rich in minerals, the kind of fact that one can find in any tourist leaflet – but I'm not in the least interested. Then we stop outside what looks like a huge Orthodox church.

'This is the Cathedral of Blood, built on the site of a house owned by a man called Nikolai Ipatiev. Let's go inside.'

I'm starting to feel cold and so I do as he suggests. We go into what appears to be a small museum, in which all the notices are in Russian.

Aleph

Yao looks at me, as if I should know what's going on, but I don't.

'Don't you feel anything?'

'No,' I say. He seems disappointed.

'You mean that you, a man who believes in parallel worlds and in the eternity of the present moment, feel absolutely nothing?'

I feel tempted to tell him that what brought me to Russia in the first place was a conversation with J. about precisely that, my inability to connect with my spiritual side. Except that this is no longer true. Since I left London, I've been a different person, feeling calm and happy on my journey back to my kingdom and my soul. For a fraction of a second, I remember the episode on the train and Hilal's eyes, but quickly drive the memory from my mind.

'The fact that I can't feel anything doesn't necessarily mean that I'm disconnected. Perhaps my energies at this moment are alert to other discoveries. We're in what seems to be a recently built cathedral. What exactly happened here?'

'The Russian Empire ended in the house of Nikolai Ipatiev. On the night of 16 July 1918, the family of Nicholas II, the last Tsar of all the Russias, was executed along with his doctor and three servants. They started with the Tsar himself, who received several bullets in the head and chest. The last to die were Anastasia, Tatiana, Olga and Maria, who were bayoneted to death.

It's said that their ghosts continue to haunt this place, looking for the jewels they left behind. People also say that Boris Yeltsin, when he was President of Russia, decided to demolish the old house and build a church in its place, so that the ghosts would leave and Russia could begin to grow again.'

'Why did you bring me here?'

For the first time since we met in Moscow, Yao seems embarrassed.

'Because yesterday, you asked me if I believed in God. Well, I did believe until He took away my wife, the person I loved most in the world. I always thought I would die before her, but that isn't what happened,' Yao tells me. 'The day we met, I felt certain that I'd known her since before I was born. It was raining heavily and she declined my invitation to tea, but I knew then that we were like the clouds that fill the sky so that you can no longer tell where one ends and another begins. We married a year later, as if it were the most obvious and natural thing in the world to do. We had children, we honoured God and family, then, one day, a wind came and parted the clouds.'

I wait for him to finish what he has to say.

'It's not fair. It wasn't fair. It may seem absurd, but I would have preferred it if we had all departed together for the next life, like the Tsar and his family.'

No, he has still not said everything he wants to. He's waiting for me to say something, but I remain silent. It seems that the ghosts of the dead really are there with us.

'And when I saw you and the young woman looking at each other on the train, in the vestibule between the carriages, I remembered my wife and the first glance we ever exchanged, and how even before we spoke, something was telling me:"We're together again."That's why I wanted to bring you here, to ask if you can see what we cannot see, if you know where she is now.'

So he had witnessed the moment when Hilal and I entered the Aleph.

I look around the room again, thank him for having brought me there and ask if we can continue our walk.

'Don't make that young woman suffer,' he says. 'Whenever I see her looking at you, it seems to me that you must have known each other for a long time.'

I think to myself that this really isn't something I should concern myself with.

'You asked me on the train if I would like to go somewhere with you tonight. Is that offer still open?' I ask. 'We can talk more about all this later. If you had ever seen me watching my wife sleeping, you would be able to read my eyes and understand why we've been married for nearly thirty years.'

*   *   *

Walking is doing wonders for body and soul. I'm completely focused on the present moment, for that is where all signs, parallel worlds and miracles are to be found. Time really doesn't exist. Yao can speak of the Tsar's death as if it had happened yesterday and show me the wounds of his love as if they had appeared only minutes before, while I remember the platform at Moscow station as if it belonged to the distant past.

We sit down in a park and watch the people passing. Women with children, men in a hurry, boys standing around a radio blasting out music, girls gathered opposite them talking animatedly about something utterly unimportant, and older people wearing long winter coats, even though it's spring. Yao buys us a couple of hot dogs and rejoins me.

'Is it difficult to write?' he asks.

'No. Is it difficult to learn so many foreign languages?'

'No, not really. You just have to pay attention.'

'Well, I pay attention all the time, but I've never got beyond what I learned as a boy.'

'And I've never tried to write because, as a child, I was told that I'd have to study really hard, read lots of boring books and mix with intellectuals. And I hate intellectuals.'

I don't know if this remark is intended for me or not. I have my mouth full of hot dog and so don't reply. I think again about Hilal and the Aleph. Perhaps she found the experience so alarming that she's gone home and decided not to continue the journey. A few months ago, I would have been driven frantic if a process like this had failed to run its full course, believing that my entire apprenticeship depended on it. But it's a sunny day, and if the world seems to be at peace, that's because it is.

'What do you need in order to be able to write?' Yao asks.

'To love. As you loved your wife, or, rather, as you love your wife.'

'Is that all?'

'You see this park? There are all kinds of stories here, and even though they've been told many times, they still deserve to be told again. The writer, the singer, the gardener, the translator, we are all a mirror of our time. We all pour our love into our work. In my case, obviously, reading is very important, but anyone who puts all his faith in academic tomes and creative writing courses is missing the point: words are life set down on paper. So seek out the company of others.'

'Whenever I saw those literature courses at the university where I taught, it all seemed to me so ...'

'... artificial?' I ask, completing his sentence. 'No one can learn to love by following a manual and no one can learn to write by following a course. I'm not telling you to seek out other writers, but to find people with different skills from yourself, because writing is no different from any other activity done with joy and enthusiasm.'

'What about writing a book about the last days of Nicholas II?'

'It's not a subject that really interests me. It's an extraordinary story, but for me, writing is, above all, about discovering myself. If I had to give you one piece of advice it would be this: don't be intimidated by other people's opinions. Only mediocrity is sure of itself, so take risks and do what you really want to do. Seek out people who aren't afraid of making mistakes and who, therefore, do make mistakes. Because of that, their work often isn't recognised, but they are precisely the kind of people who change the world and, after many mistakes, do something that will transform their own community completely.'

'Like Hilal.'

'Yes, like Hilal. But let me say one thing: what you felt for your wife, I feel for mine. I'm no saint and I have no intention of becoming one, but, to use your image, we were two clouds and now we are one. We were two ice cubes that the sunlight melted and now we are the same free-flowing water.'

'And yet, when I walked past and saw the way you and Hilal were looking at each other ...'

I don't respond, and he lets the matter drop.

In the park, the boys never look at the girls standing just a few metres from them, even though the two groups are clearly fascinated by each other. The older people walk past, thinking about their childhood.

Aleph

Mothers smile at their children as if they were all future artists, millionaires, presidents of the Republic. The scene before us is a synthesis of human behaviour.

'I've lived in many countries,' says Yao. 'And obviously, I've been through some difficult times, known injustice, and fallen flat on my face when everyone expected the best from me. But those memories have no relevance to my life. The important things that stay are the moments spent listening to people singing, telling stories, enjoying life. I lost my wife twenty years ago, and yet it seems like yesterday. She's still here, sitting on this bench with us, remembering the happy times we had together.'

Yes, she's still here, and I would explain that to him if I could find the words.

My emotions have been very close to the surface ever since I saw the Aleph and understood what J. meant. I don't know if I'm going to be able to solve this problem, but at least I'm aware that it exists.

'It's always worth telling a story, even if only to your family. How many children do you have?'

'Two sons and two daughters. But they're not interested in my stories. They say they've heard them all before. Are you going to write a book about your trip on the Trans-Siberian railway?'

'No.'

Even if I wanted to, how could I describe the Aleph?

The Aleph

The omnipresent Hilal has still not reappeared.

After keeping my feelings to myself throughout most of the supper, saying how well the signing session went and thanking everyone for that and for the Russian music and dance put on for me at the party afterwards (bands in Moscow and in other countries always tended to stick to an international repertoire), I finally ask if anyone had remembered to give her the address of the restaurant.

They stare at me in amazement. Of course they hadn't! They all thought I was finding the girl a real pest. It was just lucky she didn't turn up during the signing session.

'She might have given another of her violin recitals, hoping to steal the limelight again,' says my editor.

Yao is watching me from the other side of the table. He knows that I mean the exact opposite, and that I would love her to be here. But why? So that I could visit the Aleph again and go through a door that only ever brings me bad memories? I know where that door leads.

I've been through it four times before and have never been able to find the answer I need. That isn't what I came looking for when I began the long journey back to my kingdom.

We finish supper. The two readers' representatives, chosen at random, take photographs and ask if I would like them to show me the city. I tell them, yes, I would.

'We already have a date,' says Yao.

My publishers' irritation, previously directed at Hilal and her insistence on being with me all the time, is now turned on my interpreter, whom they employed and who is now demanding my presence, when it should be the other way round.

'I think Paulo's tired,' says my publisher. 'It's been a long day.'

'He's not tired. His energy levels are fine after all the loving vibes from this evening.'

My publishers are right about Yao. He does seem to want to show everyone that he occupies a privileged position in 'my kingdom'. I understand his sadness at losing the woman he loved and, when the moment comes, I'll find the right words to say this. I'm afraid, though, that what he wants is to tell me 'an amazing story that would make a fantastic book'. I've heard this many times before, especially from people who have lost someone they love.

I decide to try and please everyone:

'I'll walk back to the hotel with Yao. After that, I need a bit of time alone.' This will be my first night alone since we set off.

The temperature has dropped more than we imagined, the wind is blowing and it feels intensely cold. We walk along a crowded street and I see that I'm not the only one wanting to head straight home. The doors of the shops are closing, the chairs are already piled up on the tables, and the neon lights are starting to go out. Even so, after a day and a half shut up in a train and knowing that we still have many, many kilometres ahead of us, I need to take every opportunity to do some physical exercise.

Yao stops next to a van selling drinks and asks for two orange juices. I don't particularly want to drink anything, but perhaps a little vitamin C would be a good idea in this cold weather.

'Keep the cup.'

I don't quite know what he means, but I do as he says. We continue walking down what must be the main street in Ekaterinburg. At one point, we stop outside a cinema.

'Perfect. With your hood and scarf on, no one will recognise you. Let's do a little begging.'

'Begging?! Look, I haven't done that since my hippie days, and besides, it would be an insult to people who are in real need.'

'But you are in real need. When we visited the Ipatiev House, there were moments when you simply weren't there, when you seemed distant, trapped in the past, constrained by everything you've achieved and that you're doing your best to cling on to. I'm worried about the girl too, but if you really want to change, then begging will help you become more innocent, more open.'

I *am* worried about Hilal, but I tell him that – while I understand what he's saying – one of my many motives for making this trip is to travel back into the past, into what lies underground, to my roots.

I'm about to tell him about the Chinese bamboo, but decide against it.

'You're the one who's trapped by time. You refuse to accept that your wife is dead, which is why she's still here by your side, trying to console you, when, by now, she should be moving on towards an encounter with the Divine Light. No one ever loses anyone. We are all one soul that needs to continue growing and developing in order for the world to carry on and for us all to meet once again. Sadness really doesn't help.'

He thinks about what I've said, then says:

'But that can't be the whole answer.'

'No, it's not,' I agree. 'When the time is right, I'll explain more fully. Now let's go back to the hotel.'

Yao holds out his cup and starts asking for money from passers-by. He suggests that I do the same.

'Some Zen Buddhist monks in Japan told me about *Takuhatsu*: the begging pilgrimage. As well as helping the monasteries, which depend for their existence on donations, it teaches the student monk humility. It has another purpose too, that of purifying the town in which the monk lives. This is because, according to Zen philosophy, the giver, the beggar and the alms money itself all form part of an important chain of equilibrium. The person doing the begging does so because he's needy, but the person doing the giving also does so out of need. The alms money serves as a link between these two needs, and the atmosphere in the town improves because everyone is able to act in a way in which he or she needed to act. You are on a pilgrimage, and it's time to do something for the cities you visit.'

I'm so surprised I don't know what to say. Realising that he may have gone too far, Yao starts putting his plastic cup back in his pocket.

'No,' I say, 'it's a really good idea!'

For the next ten minutes we stand there, on opposite pavements, shifting from foot to foot to stave off the cold, our cups held out to the people who pass. At first, I say nothing, but gradually lose my inhibitions and start asking for help, as a poor lost stranger.

I've never felt awkward about asking. I've known lots of people who care about others and are extremely generous when it comes to giving and who feel real pleasure when someone asks them for advice or help.

And that's fine; it's a good thing to help your neighbour. On the other hand, I know very few people capable of receiving, even when the gift is given with love and generosity. It's as if the act of receiving made them feel inferior, as if depending on someone else were undignified. They think: If someone is giving us something, that's because we're incapable of getting it for ourselves. Or else: The person giving me this now will one day ask for it back with interest. Or even worse: I don't deserve to be treated well.

But those ten minutes remind me of the person I was, they educate me, free me. In the end, when I cross the street to join Yao, I have the equivalent of eleven dollars in my plastic cup. Yao has about the same amount. And contrary to what he thought, it had been a really enjoyable return to the past for me, reliving something I hadn't experienced in ages and thus renewing not only the city, but myself.

'What shall we do with the money?' I ask.

My view of him is beginning to shift again. He knows some things and I know others, and there's no reason why we can't continue this mutual learning experience.

'In theory, it's ours, because it was given to us, but it's best to keep it somewhere separate and spend it on something you think is important.'

I put the coins in my left pocket, intending to do exactly that. We walk quickly back to the hotel because the time we've spent outside has burned up all the calories we consumed at supper.

When we reach the lobby, the omnipresent Hilal is waiting for us. A very pretty woman and a gentleman in a suit and tie stand next to her.

'Hello,' I say to Hilal. 'I understand that you've gone back home, but it's been a pleasure to have travelled this first leg of the journey with you. Are these your parents?'

The man does not react, but the pretty woman laughs.

'If only we were! She's a prodigy, this girl. It's a shame she can't spend more time on her vocation though. The world is missing out on a great artist!'

Hilal appears not to have heard this remark. She turns to me and says:

'"Hello"? Is that all you've got to say to me after what happened on the train?'

The woman looks shocked. I can imagine what she's thinking: What exactly happened on the train? And don't I realise that I'm old enough to be Hilal's father?

Yao says that it's time he went up to his room. The man in the suit and tie remains impassive, possibly because he doesn't understand English.

'Nothing happened on the train, at least not the kind of thing you're imagining. And as for you, Hilal, what were you expecting me to say? That I missed you? I spent all day worrying about you.'

The woman translates this for the man in the suit and tie, and everyone smiles, including Hilal. She has understood from my response that I really had missed her, since I had said so quite spontaneously.

I ask Yao to stay a little longer because I don't know where this conversation is going to lead. We sit down and order some tea. The woman introduces herself as a violin teacher and explains that the gentleman with them is the director of the local conservatoire.

'I think Hilal's wasting her talents,' says the teacher. 'She's so unsure of herself. I've told her this over and over and I'll say it again now. She has no confidence in what she does. She thinks no one recognises her worth, that people dislike the things she plays. But it isn't true.'

Hilal unsure of herself? I have rarely met anyone more determined.

'And like all sensitive people,' continues the teacher, fixing me with her gentle, placatory eyes, 'she is a little, shall we say, unstable.'

'Unstable!' says Hilal loudly. 'That's a polite way of saying "mad"!'

The teacher turns affectionately towards her and then back to me, expecting me to say something. I say nothing.

'I know that you can help her. I understand that you heard her playing the violin in Moscow, and that she was applauded there. That gives you some idea of just how talented she is, because people in Moscow are very discerning when it comes to music. Hilal is very disciplined and works harder than most. She's already played with large orchestras here in Russia and has travelled abroad with one of them. Suddenly, though, something seems to have happened, and she can't seem to make any more progress.'

I believe in this woman's tender concern for Hilal. I think she really does want to help her, and all of us. But those words – 'suddenly, though, something seems to have happened, and she can't seem to make any more progress' – echo in my heart. I am here for that same reason.

The man in the suit and tie does not speak. He must be there to provide moral support for the talented young violinist and the lovely woman with the gentle eyes. Yao pretends to be concentrating on his tea.

'But what can I do?'

'You know what you can do. She's not a child any more, but her parents are worried about her. She can't just abandon her professional career in the middle of rehearsals to follow an illusion.'

She pauses, realising that she has not said quite the right thing.

'What I mean is, she can travel to the Pacific coast whenever she likes, but not now, when we're rehearsing for a concert.'

I agree. It doesn't matter what I say. Hilal will do exactly as she wants. I wonder if she brought these two people here to put me to the test, to find out if she really is welcome or if she should stop the journey now.

'Thank you very much for coming to see me. I respect your concern and your commitment to music,' I say, getting up. 'But I wasn't the one who invited Hilal along on the journey. I didn't pay for her ticket. I don't even really know her.'

Hilal's eyes say 'Liar', but I go on:

'So if she's on the train heading to Novosibirsk tomorrow, that's not my responsibility. As far as I'm concerned, she can stay here, and if you can convince her to do so, I and many other people on the train will be most grateful.'

Yao and Hilal burst out laughing.

The pretty woman thanks me, says that she understands my situation completely and will talk to Hilal further and explain a little more about the realities of life. We all say goodbye, and the man in the suit and tie shakes my hand, smiles and, for some reason, I have the distinct impression that he would love Hilal to continue her journey. She must be a problem for the whole orchestra.

Yao thanks me for a very special evening and goes up to his room. Hilal doesn't move.

'I'm going to bed,' I say. 'You heard the conversation. I really don't know why you went back to the conservatoire. Was it to ask permission to continue the journey or to make your colleagues jealous by telling them that you were travelling with us?'

'I went there to find out if I really exist. After what happened on the train, I'm not sure of anything any more. What *was* that?'

I know what she means. I remember my first experience of the Aleph, which happened completely by chance in the Dachau concentration camp, in Germany, in 1982. I felt completely disoriented for days afterwards, and if my wife hadn't told me otherwise, I would have assumed that I'd suffered some kind of stroke.

'What happened exactly?' I ask.

'My heart started pounding furiously and I felt as if I were no longer in this world. I was in a state of total panic and thought I might die at any moment. Everything around me seemed strange, and if you hadn't grabbed me by the arm, I don't think I would have been able to move. I had a sense that very important things were appearing before my eyes, but I couldn't understand any of them.'

I feel like telling her: 'Get used to it.'

'The Aleph,' I say.

'Yes, at some point during that seemingly endless trance, unlike anything I've ever experienced before, I heard you say that word.'

Simply recalling what happened has filled her with fear again. It's time to seize the moment:

'Do you think you should continue the journey?'

'Oh, yes, more than ever. Terror has always fascinated me. You remember the story I told at the embassy—'

I ask her to go to the bar and order some coffee – I send her on her own because we're the only customers left, and the barman must be itching to turn out the lights. She has a little trouble persuading him, but returns at last with two cups of Turkish coffee. Like most Brazilians, I never worry about drinking strong black coffee late at night: whether or not I have a good night's sleep depends on other things.

'There's no way of explaining the Aleph, as you yourself saw, but in the magical Tradition it presents itself in one of two ways. The first is as a point in the universe that contains all other points, present and past, large and small. You normally come across it by chance, as we did on the train. For this to happen, the person, or persons, has to be in the actual place where the Aleph exists. We call that a small Aleph.'

'Do you mean that anyone who got into the carriage and stood in that particular place would feel what we felt?'

'If you'll let me finish, you might understand. Yes, they will, but not as we experienced it. You've doubtless been to a party and found that you felt much better and safer in one part of the room than in another. That's just a very pale imitation of what the Aleph is, but everyone experiences the Divine energy differently. If you can find the right place to be at a party that energy will help you feel more confident and more present. If someone else were to walk past that point in the carriage, he would have a strange sensation, as if he suddenly knew everything, but he wouldn't stop to examine that feeling, and the effect would immediately vanish.'

'How many of these points exist in the world?'

'I don't know exactly, but probably millions.'

'What's the second way it reveals itself?'

'Let me finish what I was saying first. The example I gave you of the party is just a comparison. The small Aleph always appears by chance. You're walking down a street or you sit down somewhere and suddenly the whole universe is there. The first thing you feel is a terrible desire to cry, not out of sadness or happiness but out of pure excitement. You know that you are *understanding* something that you can't even explain to yourself.'

The barman comes over to us, says something in Russian and gives me a note to sign. Hilal explains that we have to leave. We walk over to the door.

Saved by the referee's whistle!

'Go on. What's the second way?'

It would seem the game is not over yet.

'That's the great Aleph.'

It's best if I explain everything now, then she can go back to the conservatoire and forget all about what happened.

'The great Aleph occurs when two or more people with a very strong affinity happen to find themselves in the small Aleph. Their two different energies complete each other and provoke a chain reaction. Their two energies ...'

I don't know if I should go on, but I have no choice. Hilal completes the sentence for me:

'... are the positive and negative poles you get in any battery, the power makes the bulb light up. They're transformed into the same light. Planets that attract each other and end up colliding. Lovers who meet after a long, long time. The second Aleph also happens by chance when two people whom Destiny has chosen for a specific mission meet in the right place.'

Exactly, but I want to be sure she really has understood.

'What do you mean by "the right place"?' I ask.

'I mean that two people can spend their whole life living and working together or they can meet only once and say goodbye for ever simply because they did not pass through the physical point that triggers an outpouring of the thing that brought them together in this world. So they part without ever quite understanding why it was they met. However, if God so wishes, those who once knew love will find each other again.'

'Not necessarily, but people who had shared affinities, like my master and myself, for example …'

'… before, in past lives,' she says, interrupting me again. 'Or people who meet, like at the party you used as an example, in the small Aleph and immediately fall in love. The famous "love at first sight".'

I decide to continue the example she has used.

'Although, of course, it isn't "at first sight", but linked to a whole series of things that occurred in the past. That doesn't mean that *every* such encounter is related to romantic love. Most of them occur because of things that have remained unresolved, and we need a new incarnation in order to finish something that was left incomplete. You're reading things into the situation that aren't there.'

'I love you.'

'No, that isn't what I'm saying,' I exclaim in exasperation. 'I've already met the woman I needed to meet in this incarnation. It took me three marriages before I found her, and I certainly don't intend leaving her for someone else. We met many centuries ago and will remain together for the centuries to come.'

But she doesn't want to hear what I have to say. Just as she did in Moscow, she plants a brief kiss on my lips and sets off into the icy Ekaterinburg night.

Dreamers Can Never Be Tamed

Life is the train, not the station. And after almost two days of travelling, it's also weariness, disorientation, nostalgia for the days spent in Ekaterinburg, and the growing tensions in a group of people confined together in one place.

Before we set off again, I found a message from Yao at reception, asking if I fancied doing a bit of aikido training, but I didn't reply. I needed to be alone for a few hours.

I spent the whole morning getting as much exercise as possible, which for me meant running and walking. That way, when I went back to the train, I would surely be tired enough to sleep. I managed to phone my wife – my mobile didn't work on the train – and confided to her that I had my doubts about the usefulness of this Trans-Siberian trip, adding that, although the journey so far had been a valuable experience, I might not carry it through to the end.

She said that whatever I decided was fine with her and not to worry. She was very busy with her paintings. Meanwhile, she'd had a dream that she couldn't understand. She had dreamed that I was on a beach and someone walked up from the sea to tell me that I was finally fulfilling my mission. Then the person vanished.

I asked if that person was male or female. She didn't know, she said, their face was covered by a hood. Then she blessed me and again reassured me, telling me not to worry. Rio, she told me, was like an oven. Then she advised me to follow my intuition and take no notice of what other people were saying.

'In that same dream, a woman or a girl, I can't be sure, was on the beach with you.'

'There's a young woman with me here on the train. I don't know how old she is, but she's definitely under thirty.'

'Trust her.'

In the afternoon, I met up with my publishers and gave a few interviews, then we had supper at an excellent restaurant and at about eleven o'clock at night headed for the station. Back on the train, we crossed the Ural Mountains – the chain of mountains that separates Europe from Asia – in the pitch dark. No one saw a thing.

From then on, it was back to the old routine. When day broke, we all appeared at the breakfast table, as if summoned by some inaudible bell. Again, no one had managed to get a wink of sleep, not even Yao, who seemed accustomed to this type of journey. He was beginning to look ever wearier and sadder.

As usual, Hilal was there waiting, and, as usual, she had slept better than anyone else. Over breakfast, we began our conversation with complaints about the constant rocking of the carriage, then I went back to my room to try and sleep, got up again a few hours later, and returned to the lounge, where I encountered the same people. Together we bemoaned the thousands of kilometres that still lay ahead. Then we sat gazing out of the window, smoking and listening to the irritating piped music issuing from the train's loudspeakers.

Hilal now barely spoke. She always sat down in the same corner, opened her book and began to read, removing herself from the group. No one else, apart from me, seemed bothered by this, but I found her behaviour very rude indeed. However, when I considered the alternative – her penchant for making inappropriate remarks – I decided to say nothing.

I would finish my meal, go back to my compartment to sleep or doze or write. As everyone agreed, we were rapidly losing all sense of time. We no longer cared if it was day or night; our days were measured out in mealtimes, as I imagine the days of all prisoners are.

We would turn up in the lounge to find supper was served. More vodka than mineral water was drunk and there was more silence than conversation. My publisher told me that, when I wasn't there, Hilal played an imaginary violin, as if she were practising. I know that chess players do the same, playing entire games in their head, without the need of a board.

'Yes, she's playing silent music for invisible beings. Perhaps they need it.'

Another breakfast. Today, though, things are different. Inevitably, we are starting to get used to our new way of life. My publisher complains that his mobile phone isn't working properly (mine doesn't work at all). His wife is dressed like an odalisque, which strikes me as both amusing and absurd. She doesn't speak English, but we somehow manage to understand each other very well through looks and gestures. Hilal decides to take part in this morning's conversation and describes some of the difficulties faced by musicians struggling to make a living. It might be a prestigious profession, but many musicians earn less than taxi drivers.

'How old are you?' asks my editor.

'Twenty-one.'

'You don't look it.'

She says this in a way that implies she looks much older. And she really does. It had never occurred to me that she was so young.

'The director of the music conservatoire came to see me at the hotel in Ekaterinburg,' says the editor. 'He said you were one of the most talented violinists he's ever known, but that you had suddenly lost all interest in music.'

'It was the Aleph,' Hilal replies, avoiding my eyes.

'The Aleph?'

Everyone looks at her in surprise. I pretend not to have heard.

'Yes, the Aleph. I couldn't find it, and my energy stopped flowing. Something in my past was blocking it.'

The conversation seems to have taken a completely surreal turn. I still say nothing, but my publisher tries to ease the situation:

'I published a mathematics book with that word in the title. In technical language, it means "the number that contains all numbers". The book was about the Kabbalah and mathematics. Apparently, mathematicians use the Aleph to represent the cardinality of infinite sets …'

No one appears to be following this explanation. He stops midway.

'It's in the Apocalypse as well,' I say, as if I'd just picked up the thread of the conversation. 'Where the Lamb is defined as the beginning and the end, as the thing that is beyond time. It's also the first letter of the alphabet in Hebrew, Arabic and Aramaic.'

The editor now regrets having made Hilal the centre of attention and decides to bring her down a peg or two.

'Nevertheless, for a girl of twenty-one, just out of music school and with a brilliant career ahead of her, it must be quite enough to have travelled all the way from Moscow to Ekaterinburg.'

'Especially for someone who's a *spalla*,' says Hilal.

She noticed the confusion her use of the word 'aleph' caused and is delighted to confuse the editor still further with yet another mysterious term.

The tension grows, until Yao intervenes.

'You're a *spalla* already? Congratulations!'

Then turning to the rest of the group, he adds:

'As you all know, *spalla* is the first violin in an orchestra, the last player to come onto the stage before the conductor enters, and who is always seated in the first row on the left. He or she is responsible for making sure all the other instruments are in tune. Actually, I know an interesting story on the subject, which took place when I was in Novosibirsk, our next stop. Would you like to hear it?'

Everyone agrees, as if they had, indeed, always known the meaning of the word *spalla*.

Yao's story turns out not to be particularly interesting, but confrontation between Hilal and my editor is averted. After a tedious dissertation on the marvels of Novosibirsk, everyone has calmed down and people are considering going back to their compartments and trying to rest a little, while I once again regret ever having had the idea of crossing a whole continent by train.

'Oh, I've forgotten to put up today's thought,' says Yao.

Aleph

On a yellow Post-it he writes: 'Dreamers can never be tamed', and sticks it on the mirror next to the previous day's 'thought'.

'There's a TV reporter waiting at one of the next stations and he'd like to interview you,' says my publisher.

I say 'Fine', glad of any distraction, anything to help pass the time.

'Write about insomnia,' says my publisher. 'You never know, it might help you sleep.'

'I want to interview you too,' says Hilal, and I see that she has fully recovered from her lethargy.

'Make an appointment with my publisher,' I tell her.

I go and lie down in my compartment, then, as usual, spend the next two hours tossing and turning. My biological clock is completely out of kilter, and, like any insomniac, I assure myself optimistically that I can use the time to reflect on interesting matters, but that, of course, proves to be totally impossible.

Suddenly, I can hear music. At first, I think that my perception of the spiritual world has somehow effortlessly returned, but realise that, as well as the music, I can also hear the sound of the wheels on the track and the objects joggling about on my table.

The music is real. And it's coming from the bathroom. I go and open the door.

Hilal is standing with one foot in the shower and one foot out, balancing as best she can, and she's playing her violin. She smiles when she sees me, because I'm naked apart from my underpants. However, the situation seems to me so natural and so familiar, that I make no effort to go and put on my trousers.

'How did you get in here?'

She continues to play, but indicates with a movement of her head the door into the next compartment, with which I share the bathroom. She says:

'I woke up this morning knowing that it's up to me to help you get back in touch with the energy of the Universe. God passed through my soul and told me that if you succeed in doing that, then so will I. And He asked me to come in here and play you to sleep.'

I've never mentioned losing touch with that energy, and I'm moved by her concern. The two of us struggle to keep our balance in the constantly rocking carriage; her bow touches the strings, the strings give out a sound, the sound fills the space, the space becomes transformed into musical time, and is filled with peace and the divine light that comes from everything dynamic and alive, and all thanks to her violin.

Hilal's soul is in every note, in every chord. The Aleph had revealed to me a little about the woman standing before me. I can't remember every detail of our joint story but I know that she and I have met before. I only hope she never learns in what circumstances that meeting took place. At this precise moment, she is enfolding me in the energy of love, as she may have done in the past. And long may she continue to do so because love

114

is the only thing that will save us, independent of any mistakes we may make. Love is always stronger.

I begin to dress her in the clothes she was wearing when I met her the last time we were alone together, before other men arrived in the city and changed the whole story: embroidered waistcoat, white lace blouse, an ankle-length skirt in black velvet threaded with gold. I listen to her talking about her conversations with the birds, and what the birds have to say to mankind, even though men are incapable of hearing and understanding. At that moment, I am her friend, her confessor, her …

I stop. I don't want to open that door unless it is absolutely necessary. I have been through it four times already and it has never got me anywhere. Yes, I remember all eight of the women who were there, and I know that one day I will hear the answer that is lacking, but, up until now, this has never prevented me from moving on in my current life. The first time it happened, I felt really frightened, but then I realised that forgiveness only works if you accept it.

And that is what I did.

There is a moment in the Bible, during the Last Supper, when Jesus predicts that one of his disciples will deny him and one will betray him. He considers both crimes to be equally grave. Judas betrays him and, eaten away by guilt, hangs himself. Peter denies him, not just once but three times. He had time to think about what he was doing, but he persisted in his error. However, instead of punishing himself for this, he makes a strength of his weakness and becomes the first great preacher of the message taught him by the man whom he had denied in his hour of need.

The message of love was greater than the sin. Judas failed to understand this, but Peter used it as a working tool.

I don't want to open that door, because it's like a dam holding back the ocean. Just one small hole would be enough for the pressure of the water to destroy everything and flood what should not be flooded. I'm on a train and the only thing that exists is a Turkish woman called Hilal, who is first violin in an orchestra and is now standing in my bathroom playing her music. I'm beginning to feel sleepy, the remedy is taking effect. My head droops, my eyes are closing. Hilal stops playing and asks me to go and lie down. I obey.

She sits in the chair and continues to play. Suddenly I am not in the train, nor in the garden where I saw her in that white lace blouse; I'm travelling down a long, deep tunnel that will carry me into nothingness, into heavy, dreamless sleep. The last thing I remember before falling asleep is the phrase that Yao stuck on the mirror that morning.

*　*　*

Yao is calling me.

'The reporter is here.'

It's still daylight, and the train is standing in a station. I get up, my head spinning, open the door a crack and find my publisher waiting outside.

'How long have I been asleep?'

'All day I think. It's five o'clock in the afternoon.'

I tell him that I need a bit of time to take a shower and wake up properly so that I don't say things I'll regret later.

'Don't worry,' Yao says. 'The train will be here for the next hour.'

It's lucky that we're stationary: having a shower when the train is in motion is a difficult and dangerous task. I could easily slip and hurt myself and end the journey in the most ridiculous way possible – on crutches. Whenever I get into the shower, I feel rather as if I were surfing. Today, though, it's easy.

Fifteen minutes later, I emerge, have a coffee with the others, and then I'm introduced to the reporter. I ask him how long he needs for the interview.

'We can arrange a time. I thought I could travel with you until the next station and—'

'Ten minutes will do. Then you can get off right here. I don't want to put you to any unnecessary trouble.'

'But you're not—'

'No, really, I don't want to put you to any trouble,' I say again. I should never have agreed to do this interview;

117

I obviously wasn't thinking straight when I said 'Yes'. My objective on this journey is quite different.

The reporter looks at my publisher, who turns away and stares fixedly out of the window. Yao asks if the table is a good place for them to film.

'I'd prefer the space between the carriages, next to the train doors.'

Hilal glances at me. That's where the Aleph is.

Didn't she get tired of sitting at the same table all the time? Once she had sent me off into that place beyond time and space, did she, I wonder, stay in the compartment, watching me sleep? Well, we'll have time enough to talk later on.

'Fine,' I say. 'Set up your camera. But, just out of curiosity, why choose such a small, noisy space, when we could stay here?'

The reporter and the cameraman, however, are already heading for the end of the carriage, and we follow them.

'Why this tiny space?' I ask again while they're setting up the equipment.

'To give the viewer a sense of reality. This is where everything happens. People leave their compartments and, because the corridor is so narrow, they come here to talk instead. Smokers meet up here. For someone else it might provide somewhere to hold a secret rendezvous. All the carriages have these vestibules.'

At the moment, the space is occupied by me, the reporter, the cameraman, the publisher, Yao, Hilal and a cook who has come to watch.

'Could we have a little privacy?' I ask.

A television interview is the least private thing in the world, but the publisher and the cook leave. Hilal and Yao stay where they are.

'Could you move a little to the left?' the camerman asks.

No, I can't. That's where the Aleph is, created by the many people who have stood there in the past. Even though Hilal is keeping a safe distance, and even knowing that we would only ever plunge back into that one point if we were standing close together, I feel that it's best not to take any risks.

The camera is running.

'Before we begin, you mentioned that interviews and publicity were not the main purpose of this journey. Could you explain why you decided to travel on the Trans-Siberian railway?'

'Because I wanted to. It was a dream of mine as an adolescent. That's all.'

'As I understand it, a train like this isn't exactly the most comfortable mode of transport.'

I go onto automatic pilot and start answering his questions without really thinking. The questions keep coming, about the experience itself, my expectations, my meetings with my readers. I reply patiently, respectfully, but all the time I'm longing for it to be over. I reckon that the stipulated ten minutes must have elapsed by now, but he keeps asking questions. I make a discreet gesture with my hand, indicating that he should wind up the interview. He looks slightly put out, but continues talking nonetheless.

'Are you travelling alone?'

A warning light starts flashing. It would seem that the rumour has already started to spread. I realise that this is the only reason for this unexpected interview.

'No, of course not. You saw how many people there were around the table in there.'

'But apparently the first violinist from the conservatoire in Ekaterinburg—'

Like any good reporter, he has left the most difficult question to last. However, this is far from being the first interview I've ever done, and I interrupt him, saying: 'Yes, she happened to be travelling on the same train, and when I found out, I invited her to join us whenever she liked. I love music. She's a very talented young woman, and now and then we have the pleasure of hearing her play. Would you like to interview her? I'm sure she'd be happy to answer your questions.'

'Yes, if there's time.'

He isn't here to talk about music, but he decides not to press the point and changes the subject.

'What does God mean to you?'

Aleph

'ANYONE WHO KNOWS GOD CANNOT DESCRIBE HIM. ANYONE WHO CAN DESCRIBE GOD DOES NOT KNOW HIM.'

Wow!

I'm surprised by my own words. I've been asked this dozens of times and my automatic-pilot response is always: 'When God spoke to Moses, he said: "I am", so God is, therefore, neither the subject nor the predicate, he's the verb, the action.'

Yao comes over to me.

'Fine, we'll end the interview there. Thanks very much for your time.'

Like Tears in the Rain

I go back into my compartment and start feverishly noting down everything I've just been talking about with the others. We will soon be arriving in Novosibirsk. I mustn't forget anything, not a single detail. It doesn't matter who asked what. If I can record my responses, they will provide excellent material for reflection.

When the interview is over, I ask Hilal to go and fetch her violin, on the assumption that the reporter will stay around for a while longer. That way, the cameraman can film her, and her work will reach a wider public. The reporter, however, says that he has to leave at once and send his interview off to the editorial office.

Meanwhile, Hilal returns with her violin, which she had left in the empty compartment next to mine.

My editor reacts badly.

'If you're going to stay in that compartment, you'll have to share the cost of the hire of the carriage. You're taking up what little space we have.'

Then she sees the look in my eyes and does not pursue the topic.

'Since you're ready, why don't you play something for us?' Yao says to Hilal.

I ask for the loudspeakers in the carriage to be turned off and suggest that Hilal play something brief, very brief. She does as asked.

The atmosphere grows suddenly limpid. It must be obvious to everyone, because the constant tiredness that has been afflicting us all simply vanishes. I'm filled by a deep sense of peace, deeper even than the peace I experienced shortly before in my compartment.

Why have I been complaining all these months about not being in touch with the Divine Energy? What nonsense! We are always in touch with it, it's only routine that prevents us from feeling it.

'I need to speak, but I don't know exactly what about, so just ask me whatever you like,' I say.

It won't be me speaking, but there's no point trying to explain that.

'Have you met me somewhere in the past?' Hilal asks.

Would she really like me to answer that right there, in front of everyone?

'It doesn't matter. You need to think about where each of us is right now, in the present moment. We're accustomed to measuring time in the same way we measure the distance between Moscow and Vladivostok, but that isn't how it works. Time neither moves nor is it stationary. Time changes. We occupy one point in that constantly mutating time – our Aleph. The idea that time passes is important when you need to know when a train is going to leave, but apart from that, it's not very useful at all, not even when you're cooking. After all, however often you make a recipe, it always turns out different. Do you follow?'

Now that Hilal has broken the ice, everyone starts asking questions:

'Are we the result of what we learn?'

'We learn in the past, but we are not the result of that. We suffered in the past, loved in the past, cried and laughed in the past, but that's of no use to the present. The present has its challenges, its good and bad side. We can neither blame nor be grateful to the past for what is happening now. Each new experience of love has nothing whatsoever to do with past experiences, it's always new.'

I'm talking to them, but also to myself. I wonder out loud:

'Is it possible to fix love and make it stand still in time? Well, we can try, but that would turn our lives into a hell. I haven't been married for more than twenty years to the same person, because neither she nor I have remained the same. That's why our relationship is more alive than ever. I don't expect her to behave as she did when we first met. Nor does she want me to be the person I was when I found her. Love is beyond time, or, rather, love is both time and space, but all focused on one single constantly evolving point – the Aleph.'

'People aren't used to that way of thinking. They want everything to stay the same …'

'… and the consequence of that is pain,' I say, interrupting the speaker. 'We are not the person other people wish we were. We are who we decide to be. It's always easy to blame others. You can spend your entire life blaming the world, but your successes or failures are entirely your own responsibility. You can try to stop time, but it's a complete waste of energy.'

The train brakes suddenly, unexpectedly, and everyone is startled. I am continuing to take in the meaning of what I'm saying, although I'm not sure everyone is keeping up with me.

'Imagine that the train didn't brake in time, that there was a final, fatal accident. All those moments will be lost in time, like tears in the rain, as the android said in *Blade Runner*. But will they? No, because nothing disappears, everything is stored up in time. Where is my first kiss filed away? In some hidden corner of my brain? In a series of electrical impulses that have been deactivated? My first kiss is more alive than ever, and I will never forget it. It's here, all around me. It forms part of my Aleph.'

'But there are all kinds of problems I need to resolve now.'

'They lie in what you call the "past" and await a decision to be made in what you call the "future". They clog your mind and slow you down, and won't let you understand the present. If you rely only on experience, you'll simply keep applying old solutions to new problems. I know a lot of people who only feel they have an identity when they're talking about their problems. That way, they exist, because their problems are linked to what they judge to be "their history".'

When no one comments on this, I go on:

'It takes a huge effort to free yourself from memory, but when you succeed, you start to realise that you're capable of far more than you imagined. You live in this vast body called the Universe, which contains all the solutions and all the problems. Visit your soul, don't visit your past. The Universe goes through many mutations and carries the past with it. We call each of those mutations "a life", but just as the cells in your body change and yet you remain the same, so time does not pass, it merely changes. You think you're the same person you were in Ekaterinburg, but you're not. I'm not even the same person I was when I began talking. Nor is the train in the same place it was when Hilal played her violin. Everything has changed; it's just that we can't see it.'

'But one day, our personal time will come to an end,' says Yao.

'An end? But death is just a door into another dimension.'

'And yet, despite what you're saying, our loved ones and we ourselves will one day disappear.'

'Never. We never lose our loved ones. They accompany us, they don't disappear from our lives. We are merely in different rooms. For example, I can't see who is in the next carriage, but it contains people travelling in the same time as me, as you, as everyone. The fact that we can't speak to them or know what's going on in that other carriage is completely irrelevant. They are there. So what we call "life" is a train with many carriages. Sometimes we're in one, sometimes we're in another, and sometimes we cross between them, when we dream or allow ourselves to be swept away by the extraordinary.'

'But we can't see or communicate with them.'

'Yes, we can. Every night we shift onto another plane while we're sleeping. We talk with the living, with those we believed dead, with those who live in another dimension and with ourselves, with the people we once were and the people we will be.'

The energy is becoming more fluid, and I know I could lose the connection at any moment.

'Love always triumphs over what we call death. That's why there's no need to grieve for our loved ones, because they continue to be loved and remain by our side. It's hard for us to accept that. If you don't believe it, then there's no point my trying to explain.'

I notice that Yao is sitting now with head bowed. The question he asked me earlier is being answered.

'And what about the people we hate?'

'We shouldn't underestimate any of our enemies who pass to the other side,' I reply. 'In the magical Tradition, they have the curious name of "travellers". I'm not saying that they can do any harm here; they can't, unless you let them. Because the fact is that we are there with them and they are here with us. On the same train. The only way to solve the problem is to correct mistakes and resolve conflicts. And that will happen at some point, even though it might take many "lives" before it does. We carry on meeting and saying goodbye for all eternity. A departure followed by a return, and a return followed by a departure.'

'But you said we were part of the whole. Does that mean we don't exist?'

'No, we do exist, but in the same way that a cell exists. A cell can cause a destructive cancer to invade an organism, but equally it can send out chemical elements that produce happiness and well-being, but the cell is not the person.'

'Why are there so many conflicts then?'

'So that the world can evolve, so that the body can change. It's nothing personal. Listen.'

They are listening, but not hearing. I had better explain things more clearly.

'At this moment, the rails and the wheels of the train are in conflict, and we can hear the noise of that friction between metals. But the rail justifies the existence of the wheel and vice versa. The noise made by the metal is irrelevant; it's merely a manifestation, not a cry of complaint.'

The energy has almost gone now. The others keep asking questions, but I can't reply in a coherent manner. They all realise that it's time to stop.

'Thank you,' says Yao.

'Don't thank me. I was listening too.'

'You mean …'

'Oh, everything and nothing. You'll have noticed that I've changed my mind about Hilal. I shouldn't be saying this here, because it won't help her at all; on the contrary, some weak spirit might feel an emotion that degrades any human being, namely, jealousy. But my meeting with Hilal opened a door, not the door I wanted to open, but another. I passed into another dimension of my life, into another carriage full of unresolved conflicts. People are waiting for me there, and I have to join them.'

'Another plane, another carriage …'

'Exactly. We're stuck eternally on the same train, until God decides to stop it for reasons known only to Him. But since it's impossible for us to stay in our own compartment, we walk up and down, from one life to another, as if they were happening in succession. They're not: I am who I was and who I will be. When I met Hilal outside the hotel in Moscow, she mentioned a story I had written about a fire on the top of a mountain. There is another story about sacred fire, which I will tell you now:

'When the great Rabbi Israel Shem Tov saw that the Jews were being mistreated, he went into the forest, lit a sacred fire and said a special prayer, asking God to protect his people. And God sent him a miracle.

'Later, his disciple Maggid of Mezritch, following in his master's footsteps, went into the same part of the forest and said: "Master of the Universe, I do not know how to light the sacred fire, but I do know the special prayer; please, hear me!" And the miracle happened again.

'A generation passed, and when Rabbi Moshe-leib of Sasov saw how his people were being persecuted, he went into the forest and said: "I don't know how to light the sacred fire, nor do I know the special prayer, but I still remember the place. Help us, O Lord!" And the Lord helped them.

'Fifty years later, Rabbi Israel of Rizhin, in his wheelchair, spoke to God, saying: "I don't know how to light the sacred fire nor do I know the special prayer, and I can't even find the place in the forest. All I can do is tell this story and hope that God will hear me."'

Now it is me who is speaking, not the Divine Energy, but even if I don't know how to relight the sacred fire, or even why it was lit, at least I can tell the story.

'Be kind to her,' I say to the others.

Hilal pretends not to have heard. As does everyone else.

The Chicago of Siberia

We are all souls wandering the cosmos and, at the same time, living our lives, but with a sense that we are passing from one incarnation to another. If something touches the code of our soul, it is remembered for ever and affects whatever comes afterwards.

I gaze lovingly at Hilal, a love that is reflected through time, or what we imagine to be time, as in a mirror. She was never mine and never will be; that is how it is. We are both creators and creatures, but we are also puppets in God's hands, and there is a line we cannot cross, a line that was drawn for reasons we cannot know. We can approach and even dabble our toes in the river, but are forbidden to plunge in and let ourselves be carried along by the current.

I feel grateful to life, firstly, because it has allowed me to find her again when I needed to. I am finally beginning to accept the idea that I will have to go through that door for a fifth time, even if I still don't find the answer. I am grateful to life, too, because I was afraid before, but now I am not. And thirdly, I am grateful to life because I am making this journey.

It amuses me to see that tonight she is jealous. Despite being a brilliant violinist and a warrior in the art of getting what she wants, she is still a child and always will be, as will I and all those who really want the best that life can offer, as only a child can.

I will provoke her jealousy because then she will know what to do when she has to cope with other people's jealousy. I will accept her unconditional love because when she loves someone else unconditionally, she will know what she is dealing with.

'Some people call it the Chicago of Siberia.'

The Chicago of Siberia. Such comparisons normally ring very false. Before the Trans-Siberian railway was built, Novosibirsk had fewer than eight thousand inhabitants. Now the population has risen to over 1.4 million, thanks to a bridge that allows the railway to continue its steely, steaming onward march to the Pacific Ocean.

Legend has it that the women in Novosibirsk are the prettiest in all Russia. From what I can see, the legend appears to be true, although it would never have occurred to me to compare it with other places I have visited. Hilal, one of the local goddesses and I are standing before what seems like a complete anomaly: a gigantic statue of Lenin, the man who made the theory of communism a reality. What could be less romantic than looking at this man, whose goatee beard points to the future, but who is incapable of stepping off his plinth and changing the world?

The person who mentioned Chicago was the goddess, an engineer called Tatiana, who is about thirty or so, and who, after the party and the supper, decided to accompany us on our walk. Being back on terra firma feels rather like being on another planet. I find it hard to get used to being somewhere that doesn't move all the time.

'Let's find a bar where we can have a drink and a dance. We need all the exercise we can get.'

'But we're tired,' says Hilal.

At such moments, I become the woman I have learned to be and read between the lines. What she means is: 'You want to stay with this other woman.'

'If you're tired, you can go back to the hotel. I'll stay with Tatiana.'

Hilal changes tack:

'There's something I want to show you.'

'Show it to me, then. There's no need for us to be alone. After all, we've only known each other for ten days.'

This destroys her 'I'm-with-him' pose. Tatiana perks up, although this has less to do with me than with the natural rivalry that sometimes exists between women. She says she'll be delighted to show me the night-life in this Chicago of Siberia.

Lenin gazes impassively down on us, as if he has seen it all before. If, instead of wanting to create a paradise for the proletariat, he had opted for a dictatorship of love, things might have turned out better.

'Come with me, then,' says Hilal.

'Come with me'? Before I can react, Hilal is already striding ahead of us. She wants to turn the tables on us and thus deflect the blow, and Tatiana takes the bait. We set off along the spacious avenue that leads to the bridge.

'Do you know the city, then?' asks the goddess, somewhat surprised.

'That depends on what you mean by "know". We know everything. When I play the violin, I'm aware of the existence of ...'

She searches for the right word, then finds a term that I will understand, but that will exclude Tatiana from the conversation.

'I'm aware of a vast, powerful "information field" around me. It's not something I can control; rather, it controls me and guides me to the right chord whenever I feel unsure. I don't need to know the city; I simply have to let it take me where it wants to.'

Hilal is walking faster and faster. To my surprise, Tatiana has understood exactly what Hilal means.

'I love to paint,' she says. 'I'm an engineer by profession, but when I stand before a blank canvas, I find that every brushstroke is like a visual meditation, a journey that transports me to a state of happiness I never find in my work and which I hope never to lose.'

Lenin must often have witnessed such scenes before, the encounter of two forces in conflict over a third force that must be maintained or conquered. It doesn't take very long for those two forces to become allies, leaving the third force forgotten or, quite simply, irrelevant. I am merely the companion of these two young women, who now look as if they have known each other since childhood and are talking animatedly in Russian, oblivious to my existence. It's still cold – given that we're in Siberia, it's probably cold here all year round – but the walk is doing me good; each step raises my spirits, each kilometre is carrying me back to my kingdom. There was a moment in Tunisia when I thought this would never happen, but my wife was right: being alone may make me more vulnerable, but it makes me more open too.

I'm beginning to get tired of trailing after these two women. Tomorrow, I'll leave a note for Yao, suggesting we practise a little aikido. My brain has been working harder than my body.

We stop in the middle of nowhere, in a deserted square with a fountain in the middle. The water is still frozen. Hilal is breathing fast; if she continues to do so, she'll induce in herself a sensation of floating, a kind of artificially induced trance that no longer impresses me.

She is the master of ceremonies of some spectacle of which I know nothing. She asks us to hold hands and look at the fountain.

'All-powerful God,' Hilal begins, still breathing fast, 'send Your messengers to Your children standing here with open hearts to receive them.'

She continues with this familiar invocation, and I notice that Tatiana's hand is beginning to tremble, as if she, too, were going into a trance. Hilal appears to be in contact with the Universe, or with what she called an 'information field'. She continues to pray, and Tatiana's hand stops trembling and clutches mine. Ten minutes later, the ritual is over.

I'm not sure whether I should tell her what I think, but Hilal is so full of generosity and love, she deserves to hear what I have to say.

'What was that?' I ask.

She seems put out.

'A ritual to bring us closer to the spirits,' she explains.

'And where did you learn it?'

'In a book.'

Should I go on or wait until we're alone? Since Tatiana was also part of the ritual, I decide to go on.

'With all due respect to your researches and to the person who wrote the book, I think you've got hold of entirely the wrong end of the stick. What is the point of such a ritual? I see millions and millions of people convinced that they're communicating with the Cosmos and thus saving the human race. Each time it fails, as it always will, they lose a little bit of hope. The next new book or seminar restores their faith, but after a few weeks, they forget what they learned and hope drains away.'

Hilal is surprised. She wanted to show me something beyond her talent as a violinist, but she touched on a dangerous area, the only one in which my tolerance level is zero. Tatiana must think me very rude, which is why she speaks out in defence of her new friend:

'But isn't prayer a way of bringing us closer to God?'

'Allow me to answer with another question: "Will all your prayers make the sun rise tomorrow?" Of course not, the sun rises in obedience to a universal law. God is always close to us whether we pray to him or not.'

'Are you saying that our prayers are useless?' says Tatiana.

'Not at all. If you don't get up early, you'll never see the sun rise. If you don't pray, God may be near, but you won't feel His presence. However, if you believe that invocations like the one you just made are the only way forward, then you had better move to the Sonoran Desert in America or to an ashram in India. In the real world, God is more easily to be found in Hilal's violin.'

Tatiana bursts into tears. Neither Hilal nor I know quite what to do. We wait for her to finish crying and tell us what she's feeling.

'Thank you,' she says. 'Even though, in your opinion, it was useless, thank you. I have hundreds of wounds that

I carry around with me, and yet I'm obliged to behave as if I were the happiest person in the world. At least today I felt someone take my hand and say: you're not alone, come with us, show me what you know. I felt loved, useful, important.'

She turns to Hilal and goes on:

'Even when you said that you knew this city better than I do, the city where I was born and where I've lived all my life, I didn't feel belittled or insulted. I believed you, I wasn't alone any more, someone was going to show me something I didn't know. I have never seen this fountain before, and now, whenever I feel low, I'll come back here and ask God to protect me. I know that the words weren't anything very special. I've often said such prayers before and never been heard, and each time that happened, my faith ebbed away. Today, however, something did happen, because although you are strangers, you're not strangers to me.'

Tatiana has still not finished:

'You're much younger than me and have not suffered what I have suffered. You don't know life, but you're lucky. You're in love with a man, which is why you made me fall in love with life again. In the future, it will be much easier for me to fall in love with someone.'

Hilal lowers her eyes. This isn't what she wants to hear. Perhaps she had planned to say the same thing, but someone else is speaking these words in the city of Novosibirsk in Russia, which is just as we imagined it would be, although very different from the reality God created on this Earth.

'In short, I have forgiven myself and I feel much lighter,' Tatiana goes on. 'I don't know why you came here or why you asked me to come with you, but you have confirmed what I have always felt: people meet when they need to meet. I have just saved myself from myself.'

And the expression on her face really has changed. The goddess has become a sprite. She opens her arms to Hilal, who goes over to her. The two women embrace. Tatiana looks across at me and beckons with her head for me to join them, but I stay where I am. Hilal needs that embrace more than I do. She wanted to do something magical, but it turned out to be a cliché, and yet the cliché was transformed into magic because Tatiana was capable of transmuting that energy into something sacred.

The two women remain locked in that embrace. I look at the frozen water in the fountain and I know that it will thaw one day, then freeze, then thaw again. So it is with our hearts, which are also regulated by time, but which never stop for ever.

Tatiana takes a card out of her bag. She hesitates, then hands it to Hilal.

'Goodbye,' she says. 'I know we won't meet again, but here's my phone number. Perhaps everything I've just said is merely the product of incurable romanticism and things will soon go back to being as they were before, but it was still a very important experience for me.'

'Goodbye,' says Hilal. 'And don't worry – if I could find my way to this fountain, I'll be able to find my way back to the hotel.'

She takes my arm. We walk through the cold night, and for the first time since we met, I desire her as a woman. I leave her at the door of the hotel and tell her that I need to walk a little more, alone, to think about life.

The Path to Peace

I mustn't. I can't. And, as I say to myself a thousand times over, I don't want to.

Yao takes off his clothes and stands there in his underpants. Even though he's over seventy, his body is all skin and muscle. I take off my clothes too.

I need this exercise, not so much because of the time spent cooped up in the train, but because my desire has begun to grow uncontrollably. It's at its most intense when we're apart – when she's gone to her room or I have some professional engagement – but I know that it would not take much for me to succumb to it. That's how it was in the past, when we met for what I imagine must have been the first time; when she was far from me, I could think of nothing else, but when she was a visible, palpable presence, the demons vanished and I barely had to control myself at all.

That's why she must stay here, before it's too late.

Yao puts on his uniform of white trousers and jacket and I do the same. We head in silence to the dojo, the martial arts training place that he found after making a

141

few phone calls. There are several other people practising, but we manage to find a free space.

'The Path to Peace is wide and vast, reflecting the grand design created in the visible and invisible world. The warrior is the throne of the Divine and always serves a greater purpose.' Morihei Ueshiba said this almost a century ago, while he was developing the techniques of aikido.

The path to her body is the next door. I'll knock, she'll open the door and won't even ask me what I want, because she'll be able to read it in my eyes. She might be afraid, or she might say: 'Come in, I was waiting for this moment. My body is the throne of the Divine, it serves as a manifestation here of what we are experiencing in another dimension.'

Yao and I make the traditional bow, and our eyes change. We are now ready for combat.

And in my imagination, she, too, bows her head as if to say: 'Yes, I'm ready, hold me, grab my hair.'

Yao and I approach, we take hold of each other's jacket collar, pause for a moment and then the fight begins. A second later, I'm on the floor. I mustn't think about her. I invoke the spirit of Ueshiba. He comes to my aid through his teachings and I manage to return to the dojo, to my opponent, to the fight, to aikido and the Path to Peace.

'Your mind must be in harmony with the Universe. Your body must keep pace with the Universe. You and the Universe are one.'

142

But the force of the blow only brings me closer to her. I grab her hair and throw her onto the bed. I hurl myself on top of her, that is what the harmony of the Universe is: a man and a woman becoming a single energy.

I get up. I haven't practised aikido for years, my imagination is far off somewhere, I've forgotten how to keep my balance. Yao waits for me to compose myself; I see his posture and remember how I should place my feet. I position myself before him in the correct manner, and again we grab each other's collar.

Again it isn't Yao before me, but Hilal. I immobilise her arms, first with my hands, then with my knees. I start to unbutton her blouse.

I fly through the air again, without realising how it happened. I'm on the floor, staring up at the fluorescent lights on the ceiling, unable to understand why I've let my defences get so ridiculously low. Yao holds out a hand to help me up, but I refuse it. I can manage alone.

Once more we grab each other's collar. My imagination once more travels far from there: I'm back in bed; her blouse is now unbuttoned to reveal her small breasts and hard nipples, which I bend over to kiss, while she struggles a little with a mixture of pleasure and excited anticipation of the next move.

'Concentrate,' says Yao.

'I am concentrating.'

That's a lie, and he knows it. He may not be able to read my thoughts, but he knows that I'm not really here.

My body is on fire from the adrenaline coursing through my veins from the two falls I've suffered, and from everything else that fell along with the blows I received: her blouse, her jeans, her trainers flung to the other side of the room. It's impossible to foresee the next blow, but it's perfectly possible to act with instinct, attention and …

Yao lets go of my collar and bends my finger back, in the classic finger lock. Just one finger and the body is paralysed. One finger stops everything else functioning. I try not to cry out, but I can see stars, and the pain is so intense that the dojo seems suddenly to have disappeared.

At first, the pain seems to make me concentrate on the one thing I should be concentrating on: the Path to Peace, but it immediately gives way to a feeling of her biting my lips as we kiss. My knees are no longer pinning down her arms; her hands are grasping me hard, her nails are digging into my back, I can hear her moans in my left ear. Her teeth release their grip, her head shifts slightly and she kisses me.

'Train your heart. That is the discipline every warrior needs. If you can control your heart, then you will defeat your opponent.'

That's what I'm trying to do. I manage to extricate myself from his hold and grab his jacket again. He thinks I'm feeling humiliated; he has noticed my lack of practice and will almost certainly let me attack him now.

I have read his thoughts, I have read her thoughts, I surrender. Hilal rolls over in bed and sits astride my body, then she undoes my belt and starts to unzip my trousers.

'The Path to Peace flows like a river and because it resists nothing, it has won even before it has begun. The art of peace is unbeatable because no one is fighting against anyone, only themselves. If you conquer yourself, then you will conquer the world.'

Yes, that is what I'm doing now. My blood is circulating faster than ever, the sweat runs into my eyes so that, for a fraction of a second, I can't even see, but my opponent does not seize the advantage. In just two moves, he's on the floor.

'Don't do that,' I say. 'I'm not a child who has to be allowed to win. My fight is taking place on another plane right now. Don't let me win without having deserved the pleasure of being the best.'

He understands and apologises. We are not fighting; we are practising the Path to Peace. Again he grabs the collar of my jacket, and I prepare for a blow coming from the right, but, at the last moment, it changes direction. One of Yao's hands grabs my arm and twists it in such a way that I'm forced to my knees to avoid my arm being broken.

Despite the pain, I feel much better. The Path to Peace appears to be a fight, but it isn't. It's the art of filling up what is missing and emptying out what is

145

superfluous. I put all my energy into that, and gradually my imagination leaves the bed, the girl with her small breasts and hard nipples, the girl who is unzipping my trousers and, at the same time, stroking my penis. I am fighting with myself, and I need to win this fight at all costs, even if that involves falling and getting up over and over. The kisses never given, the orgasms never achieved, the non-existent caresses after the bout of wild, romantic, abandoned sex – all those things disappear.

I am on the Path to Peace, and my energy is being poured into that tributary of the river that resists nothing and thus follows its course to the end and reaches the sea as planned.

I get up again. I fall again. We fight for nearly an hour, completely unaware of the other people there, all of whom are equally focused on what they're doing, looking for the right position that will help them find the perfect posture in their everyday life.

Afterwards, both of us are exhausted and dripping with sweat. He bows to me, I return his bow, and we head for the showers. He beat me every time, but there are no marks on my body; to injure your opponent is to injure yourself. Controlling your aggression in order not to harm the other is the Path to Peace.

I let the water run over my body, washing away everything that has accumulated and dissolved in my imagination. When desire returns, as I know it will, I will ask Yao to find another place where we can practise aikido – even if that place is the corridor of the train – and I will rediscover the Path to Peace.

Life is one long training session, in preparation for what will come. Life and death lose their meaning, there are only challenges to be met with joy and overcome with tranquillity.

'There's a man who needs to talk to you,' says Yao, while we're getting dressed. 'I said I'd arrange a meeting, because I owe him a favour. Will you do that for me?'

'But we're leaving early tomorrow morning.'

'I mean at our next stop. I'm just an interpreter, of course, so if you don't want to meet him, I'll just tell him that you're busy.'

He isn't just an interpreter, as he well knows. He's a man who senses when I need help, even if he doesn't know why.

'No,' I say, 'that's fine.'

'You know, I have a lifetime of experience in the martial arts,' he says. 'And when Ueshiba was developing the Path to Peace, he wasn't just thinking about overcoming a physical enemy. As long as there was a clear desire on the part of the student, he could learn to overcome his inner enemy as well.'

'I haven't fought for a long time.'

'I don't believe you. It might be a while since you practised aikido, but the Path to Peace continues inside you. Once learned, we never forget it.'

I can see where the conversation is leading. I could stop it right there, but I allow him to continue. He is a man with great experience of life, honed by adversity, a man who has survived despite having to change worlds many times in this incarnation. There's no point trying to hide anything from him. I ask him to go on.

'You weren't fighting with me, but with her.'

'That's true.'

'We'll continue practising then, whenever the journey allows us to. I want to thank you, by the way, for what you said on the train, comparing life and death to moving from one carriage to another, and explaining that we do that many times in our life. I slept peacefully for the first time since I lost my wife. I met her in my dreams and saw that she was happy.'

'I was talking to myself too, you know.'

I thank him for being a loyal adversary, who would not let me win a fight I did not deserve to.

The Ring of Fire

'First develop a strategy that utilises everything around you. The best way to prepare for a challenge is to cultivate the ability to call upon an infinite variety of responses.'

I had finally got access to the Internet. I needed to remember everything I had learned about the Path of Peace.

'The search for peace is a form of prayer that generates light and heat. Forget about yourself for a while and understand that in that light lies wisdom and in that heat lies compassion. As you travel this planet, try to perceive the true form of the heavens and the earth. That will only be possible if you can stop yourself becoming paralysed by fear and ensure that all your gestures and attitudes are in keeping with your thoughts.'

Someone knocks at the door. I'm so focused on what I'm reading that, at first, I can't understand what the noise is. My first impulse is simply not to open the door,

149

but what if it's something urgent? Why else would some-one come knocking at that hour?

As I go over to the door, I realise that there is one person with enough courage to do just that.

Hilal is standing outside, wearing a red T-shirt and pyjama bottoms. Without saying a word, she comes in and lies down on my bed. I lie down beside her. She rolls over towards me and I put my arms around her.

'Where have you been?' she asks.

'Where have you been?' is not an empty question. Anyone asking it is also saying 'I missed you', 'I want to be with you', 'I need to know what you've been up to'.

I don't answer. I simply stroke her hair.

'I phoned Tatiana, and we spent the evening together,' she says in answer to a question I neither asked nor answered. 'She's a sad woman, and sadness is contagious. She told me she has a twin sister, who's a drug addict and incapable of holding down a job or a relationship. Tatiana's sadness doesn't stem from there, though, but from the fact that she's successful, pretty, desirable, enjoys her work and, although she's divorced, she's already met another man who's madly in love with her. The problem is that whenever she sees her sister, she feels terribly guilty. First, because she can't do anything to help, and second, because her victory makes her sister's defeat seem all the more bitter. In other words, we're never happy, whatever the circumstances. And Tatiana isn't the only person to think like that.'

I continue stroking her hair.

'You remember what I said at the embassy, don't you? Everyone says that I have extraordinary talent, that I'm a great violinist and that success and acclaim are assured. My teacher told you so, adding:"But she's very insecure, unstable." That's not true; I have great technique, I know where to look when I need inspiration, but that isn't what I was born for and no one will convince me otherwise. The violin is my way of running away from reality, my chariot of fire that takes me far from myself, and I owe my life to it. I survived so that I would meet someone who would free me from all the hatred I feel. When I read your books, I realised that you were that person. Of course.'

'Of course.'

'I tried to help Tatiana, saying that ever since I was a young girl, I've done my best to destroy all the men who came near me, simply because one of them tried unconsciously to destroy me. She wouldn't believe it, though. She thinks I'm just a child. She only agreed to meet me so that she could get nearer to you.'

She moves a little closer. I can feel the warmth of her body.

'She asked if she could go with us to Lake Baikal. She says that, even though the train passes through Novosibirsk every day, she has never had a reason to get on it before, but now she has.'

As I predicted, now that I'm lying here next to her, I

feel only tenderness for the young woman by my side. I turn out the light, and the room is lit by the glow from the welding torches being used on a building site opposite.

'I said she couldn't, that even if she did get on the train, she wouldn't be allowed into your carriage. The guards won't let you pass from one class to another. She thought I was just trying to put her off.'

'People here work all night,' I say.

'Are you listening to me?'

'Yes, I'm listening, but I don't understand. Another person comes looking for me in precisely the same circumstances in which you did, but instead of helping her, you drive her away.'

'That's because I'm afraid that she'll get too close to you and then you'll lose interest in me. I don't know exactly who I am or what I'm doing here, and it could all disappear from one moment to the next.'

I reach out my left hand for my cigarettes, then light one for me and one for her. I place the ashtray on my chest.

'Do you desire me?' she asks.

I feel like saying: 'Yes, I desire you when you're far away, when you're just a fantasy. Today I practised aikido for nearly an hour, thinking about you all the time, about your body, your legs, your breasts, and yet the fighting used up only a tiny part of that energy. I love and desire my wife, and yet I also desire you. I'm not the only man who desires you, nor am I the only married man ever to desire another woman. We all commit adultery in our thoughts, ask forgiveness, then do it all over again. But it isn't fear of committing a sin that keeps me from touching you, even though you're here in my arms. I don't suffer from that kind of guilt. There's something far more important now than making love to you. That's why I feel perfectly at peace lying beside you, looking at the hotel room lit by the glow from the building site next door.' However, instead I say:

'Of course I desire you. Very much. I'm a man and you're a very attractive woman. Besides, I feel a great tenderness for you, a feeling that grows with each day that passes. I admire the way you can change so easily from woman to child, from child to woman. It's like a bow touching the strings of a violin and creating a divine melody.'

The ends of our cigarettes glow more intensely as we both inhale.

'Why don't you touch me then?'

I put out my cigarette, and she does the same. I continue stroking her hair, trying to make that journey back into the past.

'I need to do something very important for us both. You remember the Aleph? Well, I need to go through the door that frightened us both so much.'

'And what should I do?'

'Nothing. Just stay by my side.'

I begin to imagine a ring of golden light moving up and down my body. It starts at my feet, goes up as far as my head and then back again. At first, I find it hard to concentrate, but gradually the ring begins to move more quickly.

'May I speak?'

Of course she can. The ring of fire is not of this world.

'There's nothing worse than being rejected. Your light finds the light of another soul and you think that the windows will open, the sun will pour in, and all your old wounds will finally heal. Then suddenly, none of that happens. Perhaps I'm paying the price for all those men I hurt.'

The golden light, which had come into being by dint of sheer imagination – a well-known way of getting back to one's past lives – is now beginning to move of its own accord.

'No, you're not paying the price for anything. Neither am I. Remember what I said on the train, about how we're experiencing now everything that happened in the past and will happen in the future. In this precise moment, in a hotel in Novosibirsk, the world is being created and destroyed. We're redeeming all our sins, if that's what we choose to do.'

Not only in Novosibirsk, but everywhere in the Universe, time beats like God's vast heart, expanding and contracting. She draws closer, and I feel her small heart beating too, ever louder.

The golden ring around my body is moving faster now. The first time I did this exercise, immediately after reading a book about 'discovering the mysteries of past lives', I was immediately transported to mid nineteenth-century France and I saw myself writing a book on the same subjects I write about now. I learned what my name was, where I lived, what kind of pen I was using, even the sentence I had just written. I was so scared that I returned at once to the present, to Copacabana, to the room where my wife was sleeping peacefully by my side. The following day I found out everything I could about the person I had been and, a week later, decided to meet myself again. It didn't work. And however often I tried, I failed every time.

I spoke to J. about it. He explained that there is always an element of 'beginner's luck', conceived by God simply to show that it's possible, but after that, the situation goes into reverse and returns to what it was before. He advised me not to try again, unless I had some really serious issue to resolve in one of my past lives, otherwise, it was just a waste of time.

Years later, I was introduced to a woman in São Paulo. She was a very successful homeopath, who had a deep compassion for her patients. Whenever we met, I felt that I had known her before. We talked about this feeling, which she said she shared. One day, we were standing on the balcony of my hotel, gazing out at the city, and I proposed doing the ring of fire exercise together.

We were both projected towards the door I had seen when Hilal and I discovered the Aleph. That day, the homeopath said goodbye to me with a smile on her face, but I never spoke to her again. She refused to answer my phone calls or to see me when I went to her clinic, and I soon realised that there was no point in insisting.

The door, however, was open; the tiny crack in the dyke had become a hole through which the water was beginning to gush forth. Over the years, I met three other women whom I also felt I had known before, but I didn't make the same mistake again and performed the ring of fire exercise alone. None of those women knew that I was responsible for some terrible event in their past lives.

The knowledge of what I'd done didn't paralyse me though. I was determined to put it right. Eight women had been the victims of that tragedy and I was sure that one of them would eventually tell me how the story had ended. I knew almost everything, you see, apart from the curse that had been put on me.

That was why, more than a decade later, I had set off on the Trans-Siberian railway, and plunged once more into the Aleph. The fifth woman is now lying by my side, talking about things that no longer interest me because the ring of fire is spinning faster and faster. No, I don't want to take her with me back to where we first met.

'Only women believe in love, men don't,' she says.

'Men do believe in love,' I say.

Aleph

I am still stroking her hair. Her heartbeat is slowing now. I imagine that her eyes are closed, that she feels loved and protected, and that the idea of rejection has vanished as quickly as it appeared.

Her breathing slows too. She moves, but this time merely to find a more comfortable position. I move as well, to replace the ashtray on the bedside table; then I fold her in my arms.

The golden ring is spinning incredibly fast from my feet to my head and back again. Then suddenly I feel the air around me vibrating, as if there had been an explosion.

The lenses of my eyeglasses are smeared. My finger-nails are filthy. The candle scarcely gives out enough light for me to make out where I am, but I can see the sleeves of the clothes I'm wearing, made of coarse fabric.

Before me is a letter. Always the same letter.

Córdoba, 11 July 1492

My dear,

We have few weapons left, but one of these is the Inquisition, which has been the target of vicious attacks. The bad faith of some and the prejudices of others would have people believe that the Inquisitor is a monster. At this difficult and delicate moment, when this supposed Reform is fomenting rebellion in homes and disorder in the streets, slandering the court of Christ and accusing it of torture and other monstrous acts, we are still the authority! And authority has a duty to impose the maximum penalty on those who harm the general good, to amputate the infected limb from the ailing body, and thus prevent others from following their example. It is therefore only right that the death sentence should be imposed on those who, by continuing to spread heresy, cause many souls to be hurled into the fires of hell.

Aleph

These women believe they are at liberty to proclaim
the poison of their evil ways, to preach lust and Devil-
worship. They are nothing but witches! Spiritual
punishments are not always enough. Most people are
incapable of understanding them. The Church must – and
does – have the right to denounce what is wrong and to
demand radical action from the authorities.

These women have come to separate husband from
wife, brother from sister, father from children. The
Church is a merciful mother, always ready to forgive, and
our one concern is that these women should repent so
that we can deliver their purified souls to the Creator
and, as if by a divine art – in which one can read the
inspired words of Christ – carefully mete out their
punishments until they confess to their rituals and
machinations, to the spells they have cast upon the city,
which is now plunged into chaos and anarchy.

This year, we managed to drive the Mohammedans back
into Africa, guided as we were by Christ's victorious arm.
They had become almost the dominant power here, but
Faith helped us win every battle. The Jews fled too, and
those who stayed will be converted, by force if necessary.

Worse than the Jews and the Moors was the treachery
of those who claimed to believe in Christ, but betrayed
us. They, too, will be punished when they least expect it;
it is only a matter of time.

Now we need to concentrate our efforts on those
who, like wolves in sheep's clothing, have so insidiously

infiltrated our flock. This is your chance to show everyone that evil will never go unnoticed, because if these women succeed, the news will spread, a bad example will have been set, and the wind of sin will become a hurricane. We will be so weakened that the Moors will return, the Jews will regroup, and fifteen hundred years of struggle for the Peace of Christ will be buried.

It is said that torture was instituted by the court of the Holy Office. Nothing could be further from the truth! On the contrary, when Roman Law made torture legal, the Church at first rejected it. Now, though, driven by necessity, we, too, have adopted it, but its use is strictly limited. The Pope gave his permission – not an order – declaring that, in very rare cases, torture could be used. That permission is restricted exclusively to heretics. In the court of the Inquisition, so unjustly discredited, our watchwords are wisdom, honesty and prudence. After any denunciation, we always allow sinners the grace of the sacrament of confession before they face the judgment of Heaven, where secrets unknown to us will be revealed. Our greatest concern is to save these poor souls, and the Inquisitor has the right to interrogate and to prescribe the necessary methods that will make the guilty confess. That is when torture is occasionally used, but only as prescribed above.

Meanwhile, the enemies of the divine glory accuse us of being heartless executioners, unaware that the

Inquisition uses torture with a moderation and a leniency unknown in the civil courts! Torture can only be used once in every trial, and so I hope you will not waste the one opportunity you have. If you do not act appropriately, you will bring discredit on the court and we will be compelled to free those who only came into this world to sow the seed of sin. We are all weak, only the Lord is strong. But He makes us strong when he bestows on us the honour of fighting for the glory of His name.

You must not hesitate. If these women are guilty, they must confess before we can deliver them to the Lord's mercy.

And even though this is your first time and your heart is full of what you judge to be compassion – but which is really nothing but weakness – remember that Christ did not flinch from whipping the money-changers from the Temple. Your Superior will show you the correct procedures, so that when the time comes, you will be able to use the whip, the wheel, and whatever else, without your courage failing you. Remember that there is nothing more merciful than death by burning; that it is the most legitimate form of purification. The fire burns the flesh but cleanses the soul, which can then rise up to the glory of God!

Your work is vital if order is to be maintained, if our country is to overcome these internal difficulties and the Church regain the power under threat from these iniquitous creatures, and if the word of the Lamb is to echo once more in people's hearts. Sometimes fear is necessary in order for the soul to find its path again. Sometimes war is necessary in order that we can finally find peace. We do not care how we are judged now, because the future will judge us and will recognise our work.

And even if the people of the future do not understand what we have done and forget that we had to be harsh in order for people to become as meek and mild as the Son of God told us we should be, we know that our reward awaits us in Heaven.

The seeds of evil must be torn from the earth before they put down roots and grow. Help your Superior to carry out his sacred duty, with no feelings of hatred for these poor creatures, but with no pity for the Evil One either.

Remember that there is another court in Heaven, and that court will demand to know how you carried out God's wishes here on Earth.

F.T.T., O. P.

Believe Even When No One Else Believes in You

We do not move all night. I wake with her still in my arms, exactly as we were before the ring of fire. My neck is stiff from lying in the same position.

'Let's get up. There's something we need to do.'

She turns over, grumbling about how the sun rises very early in Siberia at this time of year.

'Come on, let's get up. We have to leave. Go to your room, get dressed and meet me downstairs.'

The man at reception gives me a map and shows me where to go. A five-minute walk. Hilal complains because the breakfast buffet isn't yet open.

We cross two streets and find the place I was looking for.

'But this is a church!'

Yes, a church.

'I hate getting up early and I particularly hate … this,' she says, pointing up at the blue-painted onion dome topped by a gold cross.

163

The doors are open, and a few elderly ladies are going inside. I look around and notice that the street is deserted, not a car in sight.

'I need you to do something for me.'

She gives her first smile of the day. *I* am asking *her* for something. I need her.

'Something only I can do?'

'Yes, something only you can do. Just don't ask me why I want you to do it.'

I take her hand and lead her into the church. It isn't the first time I've been inside an Orthodox church, but I never know quite what to do, apart from lighting one of the slender wax candles and praying to the saints and angels to protect me. Even so, I always love the beauty of these churches, which repeat the same architectural ideal: the vaulted ceiling, the bare central nave, the lateral arches, the icons made by artists out of gold, with prayer and fasting, and before which some of the ladies who have just come in bow, then kiss the protective glass.

As always happens when we're focused on what we want, things begin to slot perfectly into place. Despite everything I experienced last night, despite still not having got beyond reading the letter, there is time enough before we reach Vladivostok, and my heart is at peace.

Hilal seems equally enchanted by the surrounding beauty. She must have forgotten that we're in a church.

Aleph

I go over to a lady sitting in a corner selling candles. I buy four, light three and place them before what seems to be an image of St George, and I pray for myself, my family, my readers and my work.

I light the fourth and take it to Hilal.

'Please just do as I say. Hold this candle.'

Instinctively, she glances around her, to see if anyone is watching. She must think that what I'm asking her to do might seem disrespectful to the church we're in. The next moment, however, she's her usual blasé self. After all, she hates churches and doesn't see why she should behave like everyone else.

The flame from the candle is reflected in her eyes. I bow my head. I don't feel guilty at all. I feel only acceptance and the ache of a remote pain happening in another dimension, a pain I must embrace.

'I betrayed you, and I want you to forgive me.'

'Tatiana!'

I put my hand over her mouth. She may be strong and talented and a real fighter, but I have to remember that she is still only twenty-one. I should have phrased it differently.

'No, it wasn't Tatiana. But please, forgive me.'

'I can't forgive you when I don't know what you've done.'

'Remember the Aleph. Remember what you felt at that moment. Try to bring into this sacred place something that you don't know, but that is there in your heart. If necessary, think of a favourite symphony and let it guide you to where you need to go. That's all that matters now. Words, explanations and questions won't help; they'll only confuse something that is already quite complex enough. Forgive me, but let that forgiveness come from the depths of your soul, the same soul that passes from one body to another and learns as it travels through non-existent time and through infinite space.

'We can never wound the soul, just as we can never wound God, but we become imprisoned by our memories, and that makes our lives wretched, even when we have everything we need in order to be happy. If only we could be entirely here, as if we had just woken up on planet Earth and found ourselves inside a golden temple, but we can't.'

'I don't see why I should forgive the man I love. Or perhaps only for one thing, for never having heard those same words on his lips.'

A smell of incense begins to waft towards us. The priests are coming in for morning prayers.

'Forget who you are now and go to the place where the person you always were is waiting. There you will find the right words and then you can forgive me.'

Hilal seeks inspiration in the gilded walls, the pillars, the people entering the church at that early hour, the flames of the lit candles. She closes her eyes, possibly following my suggestion and imagining some music.

'You won't believe this, but I think I can see a girl, a girl who isn't here any more, but who wants to come back …'

I ask her to listen to what the girl has to say.

'The girl forgives you, not because she has become a saint, but because she can no longer bear to carry this burden of hatred. Hating is very wearisome. I don't know if something is changing in Heaven or on Earth, if my soul is being damned or saved, but I feel utterly exhausted and only now do I understand why. I forgive the man who tried to destroy me when I was ten years old. He knew what he was doing, and I did not. But I felt that it was my fault, and I hated him and myself. I hated everyone who came near me, but now my soul is being set free.'

This isn't what I was expecting.

'Forgive everything and everyone, but forgive me too,' I ask her. 'Include me in your forgiveness.'

'I forgive everything and everyone, including you, even though I don't know what crime you have committed. I forgive you because I love you and because you don't love me, I forgive you because you help me to stay close to my Devil, even though I haven't thought of him for years. I forgive you because you reject me and my powers are wasted, I forgive you because you don't understand who I am or what I'm doing here. I forgive you and the Devil who touched my body before I even knew what life was about. He touched my body, but distorted my soul.'

She puts her hands together in prayer. I would have liked her forgiveness to have been exclusively for me, but Hilal is redeeming her whole world, and perhaps that is better still.

Her body starts to tremble. Her eyes fill with tears.

'Must it be here, in a church? Let's go outside, into the open air. Please!'

'No, it has to be in a church. One day we'll do the same thing outside, but today it has to be in a church. Please, forgive me.'

She closes her eyes and holds her hands aloft. A woman coming into the church sees this gesture and shakes her head disapprovingly. We are in a sacred place, the rituals are different here; we should respect the traditions. I pretend not to notice and feel relieved because Hilal, I realise, is talking with the Spirit who dictates prayers and the true laws, and nothing in the world will distract her now.

'I free myself from hatred through forgiveness and love. I understand that suffering, when it cannot be avoided, is here to help me on my way to glory. I understand that everything is connected, that all roads meet, and all rivers flow into the same sea. That is why I am, at this moment, an instrument of forgiveness, forgiveness for crimes that were committed; one crime I know about, the other I do not.'

Yes, a spirit was talking to her. I knew that spirit and that prayer, which I had learned many years ago in Brazil.

Aleph

It was spoken by a little boy then, not a girl. But Hilal was repeating the words that were in the Cosmos waiting to be used when necessary.

Hilal is speaking softly, but the acoustics in the church are so perfect that everything she says seems to reach every corner.

'I forgive the tears I was made to shed,
I forgive the pain and the disappointments,
I forgive the betrayals and the lies,
I forgive the slanders and intrigues,
I forgive the hatred and the persecution,
I forgive the blows that hurt me,
I forgive the wrecked dreams,
I forgive the still-born hopes,
I forgive the hostility and jealousy,
I forgive the indifference and ill will,
I forgive the injustice carried out in the name of justice,
I forgive the anger and the cruelty,
I forgive the neglect and the contempt,
I forgive the world and all its evils.'

She lowers her arms, opens her eyes and puts her hands to her face. I go over to embrace her, but she stops me with a gesture.

'I haven't finished yet.'

She closes her eyes again and raises her face heavenwards.

'I also forgive myself. May the misfortunes of the past no longer weigh on my heart. Instead of pain and resentment, I choose understanding and compassion. Instead of rebellion, I choose the music from my violin. Instead of grief, I choose forgetting. Instead of vengeance, I choose victory.

'I will be capable of loving regardless of whether I am
   loved in return,
Of giving even when I have nothing,
Of working happily even in the midst of
   difficulties,
Of holding out my hand even when utterly alone and
   abandoned,
Of drying my tears even while I weep,
Of believing even when no one believes in me.'

She opens her eyes, places her hands on my head and says with an authority that comes from on high.
   'So it is. So it will be.'

A cock crows in the distance. That is the sign. I take her hand and we set off back to the hotel, looking around at the city that is just beginning to wake up. She is clearly somewhat surprised by what she has said, but for me, her words of forgiveness have been the most important part of my journey so far. This is not the final step, however. I still need to know what happens after I finish reading that letter.

We arrive in time to have breakfast with the rest of the group, pack our bags and head for the train station.

'Hilal will sleep in the empty berth in our carriage,' I say.

No one makes any comment. I can imagine what's going through their minds, but I don't bother explaining that it is not at all what they think.

'*Korkmaz git*,' says Hilal.

Given the look of surprise on everyone's face, including that of my interpreter, the words are obviously not Russian.

'*Korkmaz git*,' she says again. 'In Turkish that means "he goes and is not afraid".'

Tea Leaves

Everyone seems to have grown more used to being on the train. The table in the lounge is the centre of the universe, around which we gather every day for breakfast, lunch and supper, and where we talk about life and our hopes for the future. Hilal is now installed in the same carriage as us; she shares our meals, uses my bathroom to take her daily shower, practises obsessively, and takes less and less part in discussions.

Today we're talking about the shamans of Lake Baikal, our next stop. Yao explains that he would really like me to meet one of them.

'We'll see,' I say, which translates as 'I'm not really interested.'

However, I don't think he'll be discouraged so easily. One of the best-known principles in martial arts is that of non-resistance. Good fighters use their opponent's energy and turn it back on them. So the more I waste my energy on words, the less convinced I will be of what I'm saying, and the easier it will be to get the better of me.

Aleph

'I've been thinking about our conversation before we arrived in Novosibirsk,' my editor says. 'You said that the Aleph was a point that existed outside us, but that when people really love each other, they can locate that point wherever they want. The shamans believe that they are endowed with special powers and that only they can see such visions.'

'If we're talking about the magical Tradition, the answer is yes, the Aleph is outside us. If we're talking about the human tradition, people who are in love can, at certain very special moments, experience the Whole. In real life, we tend to see ourselves as separate beings, but the Universe is only one thing, one soul. However, to invoke the Aleph, something very powerful has to happen: a huge orgasm, a terrible loss, the climax of a great conflict, a moment of ecstasy when confronted by something of rare beauty.'

'Well, there's no shortage of conflicts,' says Hilal. 'We're surrounded by them, even in this carriage.'

Having been quiet for some time, she seems to have gone back to the beginning of the journey and to be intent on stirring up a situation that has already been resolved. She won the battle and wants to demonstrate her newly acquired power. My editor knows that these words are aimed at her.

'Conflicts are for undiscerning souls,' she replies, making a generalisation that nonetheless hits its intended target. 'The world is divided into those who understand me and those who don't. In the case of the latter, I simply leave them to torment themselves trying to gain my sympathy.'

'That's funny,' says Hilal, 'I'm just the same. I've always been that way and I've always got where I wanted to get, one example being that now I'm sleeping in a berth in this carriage.'

Yao gets up. He obviously isn't in the mood for this kind of conversation.

My publisher looks at me. What does he expect me to do? Take sides?

'You don't know what you're talking about,' says the editor, looking straight at Hilal now. 'I always thought I was prepared for everything until my son was born, and then the world seemed to fall in on me. I felt weak and insignificant and incapable of protecting him. Only children believe they're capable of everything. They're trusting and fearless; they believe in their own power and get exactly what they want. When children grow up, they start to realise that they're not as powerful as they thought and that they need other people in order to survive. Then the child begins to love and to hope his love will be requited; and as life goes on, he develops an ever-greater need to be loved in return, even if that means having to give up his power. We all end up where we are now: grown-ups doing everything we can to be accepted and loved.'

Yao has returned, balancing a tray bearing tea and six mugs.

'That's why I asked about the Aleph and love,' my editor goes on. 'I wasn't talking about love between a man and a woman. Sometimes, when I watched my son sleeping, I could see everything that was happening in the world: the place he had come from, the places he would go to, the trials he would have to face to achieve what I dreamed he would achieve. He grew up, and I loved him just as much, but the Aleph disappeared.'

Yes, she had understood the Aleph. Her words are followed by a respectful silence. Hilal is completely disarmed.

'I'm lost,' she says. 'It feels as if the reasons I had for getting where I am now have completely disappeared. I could get out at the next station, go back to Ekaterinburg, devote the rest of my life to the violin, and continue to understand nothing. On the day of my death, I will ask: what was I doing there?'

I touch her arm.

'Come with me.'

I was about to get up and take her to the Aleph, to remind her why she had decided to cross Asia by train, and I was prepared to accept whatever decision she might make. I thought of the homeopathic doctor whom I had never seen again after our joint return to a past life; perhaps it would be the same with Hilal.

'Just a moment,' Yao says.

He asks us all to sit down again, distributes the mugs and places the teapot in the centre of the table.

'When I lived in Japan, I learned the beauty of simple things. And the simplest and most sophisticated thing I experienced was drinking tea. I got up just now in order to repeat the experience and to explain that, despite all our conflicts, all our difficulties, our meanness and generosity, we can still love the simple things in life. The samurai used to leave their swords outside before going into a house, sitting down in the correct posture and taking part in an elaborate tea ceremony. During that time, they could forget all about war and devote themselves to worshipping beauty. Let's do that now.'

He fills each mug with tea. We wait in silence.

'I went to fetch the tea because I saw two samurai ready to do battle, but when I returned, the honourable warriors had been replaced by two souls who understood each other with no need for soothing tea. Let us drink together anyway. Let us concentrate all our efforts on achieving Perfection through the imperfect gestures of everyday life. True wisdom consists in respecting the simple things we do, for they can take us where we need to go.'

We respectfully drink the tea that Yao has poured for us. Now that I have been forgiven, I can savour the taste of the young leaves, picked by calloused hands, dried and made into a drink that creates harmony all around.

Aleph

None of us is in a hurry; as we travel on, we are constantly destroying and rebuilding ourselves and who we are.

When we have finished, I again invite Hilal to follow me. She deserves to know the full story and to decide for herself.

We are in the vestibule between carriages. A man of about my age is talking to a woman who is standing precisely where the Aleph is. Given the special energy of that place, they might stay there for some time.

We wait for a while. A third person arrives, lights a cigarette, and joins the other two.

Hilal makes as if to go back into the lounge.

'This is *our* space. They should be in the next carriage.'

I ask her to stay where she is. We can wait.

'Why were you so aggressive, when she obviously wanted to make peace?' I ask.

'I don't know. I'm lost. Every time we stop, every day that passes, I feel more and more lost. I thought I had such a need to light that fire on the mountain, to be by your side, to help you fulfil some mission unknown to me. I thought that she would react the way she did and do everything possible to stop that happening. And I prayed for the strength to overcome all obstacles, to accept the consequences, to be humiliated, insulted, rejected and despised, and all in the name of a love I never thought could exist, but which does exist. And I've come very close to achieving that. I now sleep in the berth next to yours, which is empty because God decided that the person who was going to occupy it would drop out at the last moment. She didn't make that decision, it came from on high, I'm sure of that. Now, though, for the first time since I got on this train bound for the Pacific coast, I suddenly have no desire to carry on.'

Another person arrives and joins the group. He comes armed with three cans of beer. It looks like their conversation is going to last quite a long time.

'I know what you mean. You think you've reached the end, but you haven't. And you're quite right; you need to understand why you're here. You came to forgive me, and I want to show you why. However, words kill, and only through direct experience will you understand everything, or rather, only then will *we* understand everything, because I don't know how the story ends either, what the last line or last word will be.'

'Let's wait for them to leave then, so that we can enter the Aleph.'

'That's what I thought too, but they're clearly going to be here for a while, precisely because of the Aleph. They may not be aware of it, but they're experiencing a feeling of euphoria and plenitude. It occurred to me while I was watching them that I may need to guide you and not just show you everything all at once.

'Come to my room tonight. It's hard to sleep in this carriage anyway, but just close your eyes, relax and lie down beside me. Let me embrace you as I did in Novosibirsk. I'm going to try to reach the end of that story alone and then I will tell you exactly what happened.'

'That's what I hoped to hear. An invitation to your room. But, please, don't reject me again.'

The Fifth Woman

'I didn't have time to wash my pyjamas.'

Hilal is wearing only a T-shirt she has just borrowed from me and which covers the top half of her body, but leaves her legs bare. I can't tell if she's wearing anything underneath or not. She gets into bed.

I stroke her hair. I need to use all the tact and delicacy at my command, to say everything and nothing.

'All I need at the moment is for you to embrace me, a gesture as old as humanity itself, and which means far more than the meeting of two bodies. An embrace means I don't feel threatened by you, I'm not afraid to be this close, I can relax, feel at home, feel protected and in the presence of someone who understands me. It is said that each time we embrace someone warmly, we gain an extra day of life. So please, embrace me now,' I say.

I place my head on her breast and she holds me in her arms. I again hear her heart beating fast and realise that she's not wearing a bra.

'I would very much like to tell you what I'm about to attempt, but I can't. I've never yet reached the end, the point where all things are resolved and explained. I always stop at the same moment, just as we're leaving.'

'Leaving what?' asks Hilal.

'Just as we're leaving the square, but don't ask me to explain any further. There are eight women, you see, and one of them says something to me that I can't hear. In the last twenty years, I've met four of those women, but none could take me as far as the end of the story. You're the fifth of those women. This journey didn't happen by chance, and given that God doesn't play dice with the Universe, I now know why that story about the fire lit on a mountain made you come in search of me, although I only understood this when we entered the Aleph together.'

'I need a cigarette. Can you explain more clearly? I thought you wanted to be with me.'

We sit up in bed and light a cigarette each.

'I wish I could be clearer and tell you everything, from the point where I read the letter, which is always the first thing to appear. After that, I hear the voice of my superior telling me that the eight women are waiting for us. And I know that, at the end, one of the women says something to me, but I can't tell whether it's a blessing or a curse.'

'So you're talking about past lives, about a letter in a past life?'

That's all I need her to understand, just as long as she doesn't ask me to explain which life I'm talking about.

'Everything happens here in the present. We condemn or save ourselves here and now, all the time. We're constantly changing sides, jumping from one carriage to the next, from one parallel world into another. You have to believe that.'

'I do. I think I know what you're talking about.'

Then a train passes, heading in the opposite direction. The lit windows flash rapidly past; we hear the noise, feel the blast of air. The carriage rocks even more than usual.

'What I need to do now is to go over to the other side, which is in this same "train" called time and space. It's not hard to do. You simply have to imagine a ring of gold moving up and down your body, slowly at first and then gradually gaining speed. It worked incredibly well when we were in Novosibirsk together. That's why I'd like to repeat the experience. You embraced me and I embraced you, and the ring sent me almost effortlessly back into the past.'

'Is that all it takes? You just have to imagine a ring?'

My eyes are fixed on the computer on the little table in my berth. I get up and bring it over to the bed.

'We think that a computer is full of photos and images, a real window on the world, but the fact is that behind what we see on the screen there is nothing but a succession of zeros and ones, what programmers call binary language.

'We have a need to create a visible reality around us; in fact, if we hadn't done that, we humans would never have survived our predators. We invented something called "memory", just like on a computer. Memory protects us from danger, allows us to live as social beings, to find food, grow, pass on to the next generation everything we've learned, but it's not the main matter of life.'

I replace the computer on the table and come back to the bed.

'The ring of fire is merely a trick to free us from memory. I read something about it somewhere once. I can't remember the author's name now, but he said that it's what we do unconsciously every night when we dream: we enter our recent or remote past. We wake up thinking that we've dreamed the most ridiculous things while we slept, but that's not true. We've visited another dimension, where things don't happen exactly as they do here. We think it's all nonsense because when we wake up, we're immediately back in a world organised by "memory", which is our way of understanding the present. What we saw in our dreams is rapidly forgotten.'

'Is it really that easy to go back to a past life or enter a different dimension?'

'It is when we dream or when we deliberately provoke that state, but provoking such states isn't really advisable. Once the ring has a grip on your body, your soul floats off into a kind of no-man's-land. If it doesn't know where it's going, it will fall into a deep sleep and then it can be carried off into areas where it won't be welcome, and then it will either learn nothing or bring past problems into the present.'

We finish our cigarettes. I put the ashtray down on the chair that serves as my bedside table and ask her to embrace me again. Her heart is beating even faster.

'Am I one of those eight women?'

'Yes. All the people with whom we've had problems in the "past" keep reappearing in our lives, in what mystics call the Wheel of Time. We become more aware of this with each new incarnation, and those conflicts are gradually resolved. When everyone's conflicts everywhere cease to exist, then the human race will enter a new phase.'

'So did we cause these conflicts in the past just so that we could resolve them later on?'

'No, the conflicts were necessary for humanity to be able to evolve in a way and a direction that still remain a mystery to us. Imagine a time when we were all part of a kind of biological soup that covered the planet. Cells reproduced in the same way for millions of years, then one of them changed. At that point, billions of other cells said: "That's not right, that cell's in conflict with the rest of us."

'Meanwhile, that mutation made the other cells beside it change too. "Mistake" followed upon "mistake", and out of that soup came amoeba, fish, animals and men. Conflict was essential to evolution.'

She lights another cigarette.

'But why do we need to resolve those conflicts now?'

'Because the Universe, God's heart, contracts and expands. The motto of the alchemists was *Solve et coagula*, which means "separate and bring together". Don't ask me why, because I don't know.

'This afternoon, you and my editor quarrelled. Thanks to that confrontation, you were each able to reveal a light that the other was unaware of. You separated and came together again, and we all benefited from that. Things could have turned out quite differently: a confrontation with no positive results. In that case, the matter would have proved less illuminating or would have had to be resolved later. It couldn't remain unresolved because the energy of hatred between the two of you would have infected the whole carriage. And this carriage, you see, is a metaphor for life.'

She's not much interested in these theories.

'Begin then. I'll go with you.'

'No, you won't. You may be holding me in your arms, but you don't know where I'm going. Don't do it. Promise me you won't imagine the ring. Even if I don't find a complete solution, I promise I'll tell you where I met you before. I don't know that it was the first time this happened in all my past lives, but it's the only one I'm sure of.'

She doesn't answer.

'Promise,' I insist. 'Today, I tried to take you back to the Aleph, but there were people there. That means I must go there before you do.'

She releases me from her embrace and makes as if to get up. I hold on to her.

'Let's go to the Aleph now,' she says. 'There won't be anyone around at this hour.'

'Please, believe me. Embrace me again and try not to move too much even if you have difficulty sleeping. Let me see if I can get an answer first. Light the sacred fire on the mountain, because the place I'm going to is as cold as death.'

'I am one of the women, aren't I?' Hilal says again.

'Yes,' I say, still listening to her heart beating.

'I'll light the fire and stay here to watch over you. Go in peace.'

I imagine the ring. Her earlier forgiveness leaves me freer and soon the ring is moving up and down my body of its own accord, propelling me towards the place I do not want to go to, but to which I must return.

Ad extirpanda

I look up from the letter and observe the elegant couple before me. The man is wearing a spotless white linen shirt and a velvet jacket with gold embroidery on the sleeves. The woman has on a fur jacket, and the woollen bodice of her dress is sewn with pearls, while the high embroidered collar of her long-sleeved white blouse frames her anxious face. They are talking to my superior.

'We've been friends for years,' she says, giving a forced smile, as if she wanted to convince us that nothing has changed, that this is all a misunderstanding. 'You baptised her and set her on the path to righteousness.'

Then, turning to me, she adds:

'And you know her better than anyone. You played together and grew up together and only grew apart when you chose to enter the priesthood.'

The Inquisitor remains impassive.

The couple look at me with pleading eyes, begging for my help. I have often slept in their house and eaten their food. They took me in after my parents died from the plague. I nod in agreement. I am five years older, but it's true that I know her better than anyone. We did indeed play together and grow up together and, before I entered the Dominican Order, she was the woman with whom I would have liked to spend the rest of my days.

'We're not talking about her friends,' it is her father's turn to address the Inquisitor, and the smile on his face is equally false. 'I don't know what they do or what they have done. I believe the Church has a duty to put an end to heresy, just as it put an end to the threat from the Moors. These women must be guilty, because the Church is never unjust, but you both know that our daughter is innocent.'

The Order's superiors had visited the town the previous day, for their yearly visit. All the inhabitants had gathered in the main square. They were under no obligation to do this, but anyone who failed to appear was immediately viewed as suspect. Families of all social classes crowded together in front of the church, and one of the superiors read out a document, explaining the reason for the visit: to unmask heretics and lead them to earthly and divine justice. Then came the moment of mercy, when people who felt they had shown a lack of respect for divine dogma could confess spontaneously to their sins and receive only a mild punishment. However, despite the terror in everyone's eyes, no one moved.

Then the crowd was asked to denounce any suspicious activities. A farm labourer had stepped forward and named each of the eight girls. He was a man known to beat his own daughters, but who always attended Sunday mass, as if he were an innocent lamb of God.

The Inquisitor turns to me and nods, and I immediately hold out the letter to him. He places it next to a pile of books.

The couple wait. Despite the cold, the father's forehead is shiny with sweat.

'None of our family took a step forwards because we are God-fearing people. We haven't come here to save all the girls; we just want our daughter back. I promise by all that's holy that we'll send her straight to a convent as soon as she's sixteen. Her body and soul will have but one goal, devotion to the Divine Majesty.'

'That man made his accusation in front of the whole town,' the Inquisitor says at last. 'He risks public disgrace if he is found to be lying. Most denunciations are made anonymously. Such bravery is rare.'

Relieved that the Inquisitor has, at least, broken his silence, the girl's father thinks that perhaps there is a chance to negotiate.

'He's an enemy of mine, you know that. I dismissed him from his job because he coveted my daughter. It's pure revenge on his part and nothing to do with faith.'

He would like to add that the same is true of the other seven accused. There are rumours that this same farm labourer has had sexual relations with two of his own daughters. He's a pervert, who can only find pleasure in sex with young girls.

The Inquisitor removes a book from a pile on the table.

'I would like to believe that, and I'm prepared to be shown that this is the case, but I have to follow the correct procedures. If she is innocent, she has nothing to fear. Nothing, absolutely nothing will be done that is not written down here. True, we did commit certain excesses at the beginning, but we are more organised and more careful. No one ever dies at our hand now.'

He holds out the book: *Directorium Inquisitorum*. The girl's father takes it, but does not open it. He grips it hard, as if to conceal the fact that his hands are trembling.

'It contains our code of conduct,' the Inquisitor goes on. 'The roots of the Christian faith. The perverse ways of heretics. And how we should distinguish one from the other.'

The woman raises one hand to her mouth, trying to bite back her fear and her tears. She sees that they will achieve nothing here.

'I won't be the one to go to the court and tell how, as a child, she used to talk to what she called her "invisible friends". It's well known in the town that she and her friends would go down to the woods and sit around an upturned glass, place their fingers on it and try to make it move by dint of sheer willpower. Four of them have confessed to having tried to enter into contact with the spirits of the dead in order that they might know the future, and to having diabolical powers, such as the ability to converse with what they call "the forces of nature". God is the only force and the only power.'

'But all children do such things!'

The Inquisitor gets up, comes over to my desk, picks up another book and starts leafing through it. Despite the friendship that binds him to this family – which is the only reason he agreed to this meeting – he wants to have the matter settled by Sunday. I try to reassure the couple as best I can with my eyes, the only means open to me, given that I am with my superior and cannot voice an opinion.

They don't notice, however, being entirely focused on the Inquisitor's every gesture.

'Please,' says the mother, making no attempt now to hide her despair. 'Spare our daughter. If her friends confessed, it was only because they were—'

Her husband grabs her hand, interrupting her, but the Inquisitor completes her remark:

'Tortured? Look, we have known each other for many years, you and I, and have discussed all aspects of theology. Surely you know that God is in each of these girls and would never allow them to suffer or to confess to anything that was not true. Do you think that a little pain would be enough to extract from their souls the very worst of ignominies? His Holiness the Pope Innocent IV gave torture the seal of approval over two hundred years ago with his papal bull, *Ad extirpanda*. We do not torture because it gives us pleasure, we use it as a test of faith. Those who have nothing to confess will be comforted and protected by the Holy Spirit.'

The couple's lavish clothes are in marked contrast to the bare room stripped of all comfort, apart from a fire that has been lit to warm the place a little. A ray of sunlight enters through a chink in the stone wall and sets the jewels of the woman's rings and necklace glittering.

'This isn't the first time the Holy Office has visited the town,' says the Inquisitor. 'On previous visits, neither of you complained or thought that what we were doing was unjust. On the contrary, over supper, you approved of this practice, saying that it was the only way to stop the forces of evil spreading. Whenever we purged the town of its heretics, you applauded. You saw that we are not cruel tyrants, but seekers after truth, which is not always as transparent as it should be.'

'But—'

'But those things happened to other people, to those whom you deemed deserving of torture and the pyre. Once,' he points at the man, 'you yourself denounced a family who were neighbours of yours. You said that the mother practised the black arts and caused your cattle to die. When we proved this to be true, they were condemned and …'

He pauses before completing the sentence, as if savouring the words.

'… and I helped you to buy that family's lands for next to nothing. Your piety was well rewarded.'

He turns to me:

'Bring me the *Malleus Maleficarum*.'

I go over to the shelf behind his desk. He is a good man, convinced that he is doing the right thing. He is not carrying out some personal revenge; he is working in the name of his faith. Although he has never confessed his feelings to me, I have often seen him gazing off into the distance, as if asking God why He has placed such a heavy burden on his shoulders.

I hand him the thick, leather-bound volume, with the title emblazoned on the front.

'It's all in here, in the *Malleus Maleficarum*, a long, detailed investigation into the universal conspiracy to bring back paganism, the belief in nature as our one salvation, the superstitious belief in the existence of past lives, the vile art of astrology and the so-called "science" that denies the mysteries of faith. The Devil knows he cannot work alone, that he needs witches and scientists to seduce and corrupt the world.

'While the men are away fighting and dying in wars to defend the Faith and the Kingdom, the women start thinking that they were born to govern, and the cowards who believe themselves to be sages turn to mediums and scientific theories for what they could easily find in the Bible. It is up to us to prevent this happening. I did not bring these girls here. I am simply charged with ascertaining if they are innocent or if they must be saved.'

He gets up and asks me to go with him.

'I must leave now. If your daughter is innocent, she will be at home with you before a new day dawns.'

The woman throws herself on the ground and kneels at his feet.

'Please! You held her in your arms when she was just a baby.'

The man plays his last card.

'I will give all my lands and all my wealth to the Church, right now. Give me a pen and some paper and I will sign. I want to leave here hand-in-hand with my daughter.'

The Inquisitor pushes the woman away, but she remains kneeling, sobbing helplessly, her face buried in her hands.

'The Dominican Order was chosen precisely so that this kind of thing would not happen. The old inquisitors were easily bribed, but we Dominicans have always lived from begging and will continue to do so. Money does not tempt us; on the contrary, your scandalous offer only makes your daughter's situation worse.'

The man grabs me by the shoulders.

'You were like a son to us! When your parents died, we took you into our house, so that your uncle would not continue to mistreat you.'

'Don't worry,' I whisper in his ear, afraid that the Inquisitor might hear. 'Don't worry.'

Even though he had only taken me in so that I could work like a slave on his land. Even though he, too, had beaten and insulted me whenever I did anything wrong.

I extricate myself from his grasp and walk over to the door. The Inquisitor turns round one last time to the couple:

'One day, you will thank me for having saved your daughter from eternal damnation.'

'*U*ndress her.'

The Inquisitor is sitting at a vast table surrounded by a series of empty chairs.

Two guards make a move towards her, but the girl holds up her hand.

'I don't need them, I can do it alone. Just, please, don't hurt me.'

Slowly she removes her velvet skirt embroidered with gold thread, as elegant as the dress her mother wore. The twenty men in the room pretend to take no notice, but I know what is going through their minds: lewd thoughts, lust, greed, perversion.

'And your blouse.'

She takes off the blouse, which was doubtless white yesterday, but which is now dirty and crumpled. Her gestures seem too slow and studied, but I know what she's thinking: 'He'll save me. He'll stop this now.' And I say nothing, but silently ask God if what is happening is right. I start to repeat the Lord's Prayer over and over, asking God to enlighten both her and my superior. I know what he's thinking, that the denunciation had its roots not only in jealousy and vengeance, but in the woman's extraordinary beauty. She is the very image of Lucifer, the most beautiful and most perverse of Heaven's angels.

Everyone here knows her father, knows how power-ful he is and what harm he can do to anyone who touches his daughter. She looks at me, and I do not turn away. The others are scattered about the great subterra-nean room, hidden in the shadows, afraid that she might emerge from this alive and denounce them all. Cowards. They were summoned here to serve a great cause, to help purify the world. Why are they hiding from a defenceless young girl?

'Take off your other clothes too.'

She is still gazing fixedly at me. She raises her hands and unties the ribbon on her blue slip, which is all that is covering her body now, and lets it fall to the floor. Her eyes plead with me to stop what is happening, and I respond with a slight nod, indicating that she need not worry, everything will be all right.

'Look for the mark of Satan,' the Inquisitor tells me.

Picking up a candle, I go over to her. The nipples of her small breasts are hard, although I cannot tell whether this is because she is cold or involuntarily aroused by the fact of standing naked before all these men. Her skin is covered in goose-pimples. The tall windows with their thick glass let in little light, but the light that does enter glows on her immaculately white skin. I do not need to look very hard. On her pubis – which, when I was most sorely tempted, I often used to imagined kissing – I can see the mark of Satan hidden among her pubic hair, at the top left-hand side. This frightens me. Perhaps the

Inquisitor is right, for here is irrefutable proof that she has had sexual relations with the Devil. I feel a mixture of disgust, sadness and rage.

I need to be sure. I kneel down beside her naked body and look at the mark again: a crescent-shaped mole.

'It's been there since I was born.'

Like her parents, she thinks she can establish a dialogue and persuade everyone of her innocence. I have been praying hard ever since I came into the room, desperately asking God to give me strength. There will be some pain, but it should all be over in less than half an hour. Even if that mark is irrefutable proof of her crimes, I loved her before I gave myself, body and soul, to the service of God, knowing that her parents would never allow a noblewoman to marry a peasant.

And that love is still too strong for me to master. I do not want to see her suffer.

'I have never called up the Devil. You know me and you know my friends as well. Tell him', she points at my superior, 'that I'm innocent.'

The Inquisitor then speaks with surprising tenderness, which can only have its source in divine mercy.

'I, too, know your family, but the Church is aware that the Devil does not choose his subjects on the basis of social class, but for their capacity to seduce with words or with false beauty. Jesus said that evil comes out of the mouths of men. If the evil is within, it will be exorcised by screams and will become the confession we all hope for. If there is no evil there, then you will be able to withstand the pain.'

'I'm cold, do you think—'

'Do not speak unless spoken to,' he responds gently but firmly. 'Merely nod or shake your head. Your four friends have already told you what happens, haven't they?'

She nods.

'Take your seats, gentlemen.'

Now the cowards will have to show their faces. Judges, scribes and noblemen take their places around the large table at which the Inquisitor has been sitting alone until now. Only myself, the guards and the girl remain standing.

I would prefer this rabble not to be here. If it were only the three of us, I know that he would be moved. Most denunciations are made anonymously because people fear what their fellow townspeople will say; had this denunciation not been made in public, then perhaps none of this would be happening. But destiny has determined that things should take a different course, and the Church needs the rabble, and the legal process must be followed. Having been accused of excesses in the past, it was decreed that everything should be set down in the appropriate civil documents. Thus, in future, everyone will know that the ecclesiastical authorities acted with dignity and in legitimate defence of the faith.

Sentence is handed down by the State; the inquisitors have only to indicate the guilty party.

'Don't be afraid. I have just spoken to your parents and promised to do all I can to establish that you never took part in the rituals of which you have been accused. That you did not invoke the spirits of the dead or try to discover what lies in the future, that you never tried to visit the past, that you do not worship nature, that the disciples of Satan never touched your body, despite the mark that is clearly there.'

'You know that—'

Everyone present, their faces now visible to the prisoner, turn indignantly to the Inquisitor, expecting a justifiably stern response. However, he merely raises his finger to his lips, asking her once again to respect the court.

My prayers are being heard. I ask God to fill my superior with patience and tolerance and not send her to the Wheel. No one can resist the Wheel, and so only those whose guilt is assured are placed on it. So far, none of the four girls who have appeared before the court have merited that extreme form of punishment, which involves being tied to the frame of the wheel, dotted with sharp nails and hot coals. When the wheel is turned, the prisoner's flesh is scorched and torn.

'Bring the bed.'

My prayers have been answered. One of the guards bawls out the order.

She tries to run away, even though she knows this is impossible. She runs from one side of the room to the other, hurls herself at the stone walls, rushes to the door, but is repelled. Despite the cold and damp, her body is covered in sweat and gleams in the dim light. She doesn't scream like the other girls, she merely tries to escape. The guards finally manage to hold her down and, in the confusion, deliberately touch her small breasts and the tuft of hair covering her pubis.

Another two men arrive, carrying a wooden bed, made specially in Holland for the Holy Office. Today, its use is recommended in several countries. They place it very near the table and bind the silently struggling girl. They open her legs and clamp her ankles in the two rings at one end of the bed. Then they stretch her arms above her head and tie them to ropes attached to a lever.

'I will work the lever,' I say.

The Inquisitor looks at me. Normally, this would be done by a soldier, but I know how easily these barbarians could tear her muscles, and, besides, he has already allowed me to take charge on the four previous occasions.

'All right.'

I go over to the bed and place my hands on the piece of wood that is now worn with use. The other men lean forwards. The sight of this naked girl tied to a bed, her legs spread, could be seen as simultaneously hellish and heavenly. The Devil tempts and provokes me. Tonight I will whip him out of my body and with him the thought that, right now, I want to be here, embracing and protecting her from all those leering eyes and smiles.

'Get behind me in the name of Jesus!'

I cry out to the Devil, unwittingly pressing the lever so that her body is pulled taut. She barely groans when her spine arches upwards. I ease the pressure, and her spine relaxes.

I am still praying ceaselessly, begging for God's mercy. Once the pain threshold has been crossed, the spirit grows strong. Everyday desires become meaningless, and man is purified. Suffering comes from desire, not from pain.

My voice is calm and comforting.

'Your friends have told you about this, haven't they? When I move this lever, your arms will be pulled backwards, your shoulders will come out of joint, your spine will rupture and your skin will tear. Don't force me to go that far. Simply confess, as your friends did. My superior will absolve your sins, you will be able to go home with only a penance, and everything will return to normal. The Holy Office will not revisit the town for a while.'

I glance to the side to make sure the scribe is noting down my words correctly, that the record is there for the future.

'I confess,' she says. 'Tell me what my sins are and I will confess.'

I touch the lever very gently, just enough to make her cry out in pain. Please, don't make me go any further. Help me, please, and confess at once.

'I cannot tell you what your sins are. Even if I knew them, you are the one who must declare them to the court.'

She starts telling us everything we expected to hear, thus making torture unnecessary, but she is writing her own death sentence, and I must avoid that. I pull the lever a little harder to try and silence her, but despite the pain, she continues. She speaks of premonitions, of sensing what will happen in the future, of how nature has revealed many medical secrets to her and her friends. I start to pull the lever harder, desperate to make her stop, but she continues, her words interspersed with cries of pain.

'Just a moment,' says the Inquisitor. 'Let us hear what she has to say. Slacken the pressure.'

Then turning to the other men, he says:

'We are all witnesses. The Church calls for death by burning for this poor victim of the Devil.'

No! I want to tell her to stay silent, but everyone is looking at me.

'The court agrees,' says one of the judges.

She hears this and is lost for ever. For the first time since she entered the room, her eyes change and take on a determined look that can only come from the Evil One.

Aleph

'I confess to having committed all the sins in the world. I confess to having dreamed of men coming to my bed and giving me intimate kisses. One of those men was you, and I confess that, in my dreams, I tempted you. I confess that I gathered together with my friends to conjure up the spirits of the dead, because I wanted to know if I would one day marry the man I had always dreamed of having by my side.'

She indicates me with a gesture of her head.

'That man was you. I was waiting until I was a little older before trying to lure you away from the monastic life. I confess that I wrote letters and diaries that I later burned, because they talked about the only person, apart from my parents, who showed any compassion for me and whom I loved for that reason. That person was you—'

I pull the lever harder. She cries out and faints. Her white body is covered in sweat. The guards are about to throw cold water on her face to bring her round so that we can continue to extract further confessions from her, but the Inquisitor stops them.

'There's no need. I think the court has heard enough. Cover her with her slip and take her back to the cell.'

They pick up her inanimate body along with the blue slip that was on the floor and carry her away. The Inquisitor turns to the hard-hearted men beside him.

'Gentlemen, I await confirmation of the verdict in writing, unless anyone here has something to say in defence of the accused. If so, we will reconsider the accusation.'

They all turn to look at me, some hoping I will say nothing, others that I will save her, for, as she herself said, I know her.

Why did she have to say those words here? Why did she bring up feelings that had been so difficult to overcome when I decided to serve God and leave the world behind? Why didn't she allow me to defend her when I could have saved her life? If I speak out in her favour now, the following day, the whole town will be saying that I only saved her because she said that she had always loved me. My reputation and my career would be ruined for ever.

'If just one voice is raised in her defence, I am prepared to demonstrate the leniency of the Holy Mother Church.'

I am not the only one here who knows her family. Some owe them favours, others money, others still are motivated by envy. No one will say a word, only those who owe them nothing.

'Shall I declare the proceedings closed?'

The Inquisitor, despite being more learned and more devout than me, seems to be asking for my help. After all, she did tell everyone here that she loved me.

'Only speak a word and my servant will be healed,' the centurion said to Jesus. Just one word and my servant will be saved.

My lips do not open.

The Inquisitor does not show it, but I know that he despises me. He turns to the rest of the group.

'The Church, represented here by myself, her humble defender, awaits confirmation of the death penalty.'

The men gather in a corner, and I can hear the Devil shouting ever louder in my ears, trying to confuse me, as he had earlier that day. However, I left no irreversible marks on the bodies of the other four girls. I have seen some brothers pull the lever as far as it will go, so that the prisoners die with all their organs destroyed, blood gushing from their mouths, their bodies a whole thirty centimetres longer.

The men return with a piece of paper signed by all. The verdict is the same as it was for the other four girls: death by burning.

The Inquisitor thanks everyone and leaves without addressing another word to me. The men who administer justice and the law leave too, some already discussing the latest piece of local gossip, others with their heads bowed. I go over to the fire, pick up one of the red-hot coals and place it under my habit against my skin. I smell scorched flesh, my hands burn and my body contracts in pain, but I do not move.

'Lord,' I say, when the pain recedes, 'may these marks remain for ever on my body, so that I may never forget who I was today.'

Neutralising Energy without Moving a Muscle

A heavily made-up woman in traditional dress – and who is somewhat, not to say, grossly overweight – is singing regional songs. I hope everyone is having a good time; this is a great party, and I am feeling more euphoric with every kilometre of railway track we cover.

There was a moment this afternoon when the person I used to be slumped into depression, but I soon recovered. Why feel guilty if Hilal has forgiven me? Going back into the past and reopening old wounds is neither easy nor particularly important. The only justification is that the knowledge acquired might help me to a better understanding of the present.

Ever since the last book-signing, I've been trying to find the right words to lead Hilal towards the truth. The trouble with words is that they give us the illusory sense that we are making ourselves understood as well as understanding what others are saying. However, when we turn round and come face to face with our destiny, we discover that words are not enough. I know so many people who are brilliant speakers, but are quite incapable of practising what they preach. Besides, it's one thing to describe a situation and quite another to experience it. I realised a long time ago that a warrior in search of his dream must take his inspiration from what he actually does and not from what he imagines himself doing. There's no point my telling Hilal what we went through together, because the kind of words I would have to use to describe it would be dead before they even left my mouth.

Experiencing what happened in that dungeon, the torture and death by burning wouldn't help her at all, on the contrary, it could cause her terrible harm. We still have a few days ahead of us, and I will try and find the best way to help her understand our relationship, without her necessarily going through all that suffering again.

I could choose to keep her in ignorance and not say anything, but I sense, for no logical reason I can put my finger on, that the truth will also free her from many of the things she's experiencing in this incarnation. It was no coincidence that when I noticed that my life was no longer flowing like a river down to the sea, I decided to go off travelling. I did so because everything around me was threatening to stagnate. Nor was it a coincidence that she should say she was feeling the same.

Therefore, God will have to work with me and show me a way of telling her the truth. Each day, everyone in the carriage is experiencing a new stage in their lives.

My editor seems more human and less defensive. Yao, who is standing beside me now, smoking a cigarette and watching the people on the dance floor, is doubtless glad to have refreshed his own knowledge by showing me things I had forgotten. He and I again spent the morning practising aikido at a gym he managed to find here in Irkutsk, and afterwards he said to me:

'We should always be prepared for attacks by the enemy and be capable of looking into the eyes of death so that death may light our path.'

Ueshiba has a lot of sayings intended to guide the steps of those who devote themselves to the Path of Peace. However, the one Yao chose bears directly on what I went through last night as Hilal slept in my arms, for seeing her death had illuminated my path.

Yao appears to have some way of plunging into a parallel world and keeping pace with what is happening to me. He is the person I've talked to most (I've had some extraordinary experiences with Hilal, but she speaks less and less), and yet I still couldn't say that I really know him. I'm not sure that it helped very much my telling him that our loved ones do not disappear, but merely pass into a different dimension. He still seems to have his thoughts fixed on his wife, and the only thing I can do now is put him in touch with an excellent medium who lives in London. There he will find all the answers he needs and all the signs that will confirm what I told him about the eternity of time.

Aleph

I may have made a spontaneous decision to cross Asia by train, but I'm sure that we each now have our own reason for being here in Irkutsk. Such things only happen when all the people involved have met somewhere in the past and are travelling together towards freedom.

Hilal is dancing with a young man her own age. She has had a little too much to drink and is in ebullient mood. More than once, she has come over to me tonight to tell me how much she regrets not bringing her violin. It really is a shame. The people here deserve to experience the charm and the spell cast by that great first violinist from one of Russia's most respected conservatoires.

The fat singer leaves the stage, the band continues to play, and the audience starts jumping up and down, shouting: 'Kalashnikov! Kalashnikov!' If Goran Bregovi's music wasn't so well known, anyone passing by outside would be convinced that this was some celebration party for terrorists.

Hilal and her friend are holding each other close, one step away from a kiss. My travelling companions are doubtless concerned that I'll be upset by this. But I think it's great. If only she *would* meet a single man who could make her happy and not interrupt her brilliant career, who could hold her in his arms at sunset and always light the sacred fire whenever she needed help. She deserves it.

'I can cure those marks on your body, you know,' Yao says, while we're watching the people dancing. 'The Chinese have a remedy for it.'

I know this isn't possible.

'Oh, it's not that bad. It comes and goes at ever more unpredictable intervals, but there's no cure for nummular eczema.'

'In Chinese culture, we say that it only occurs in soldiers who were burned in battle during some previous incarnation.'

I smile. Yao looks at me and smiles back. I don't know if he realises what he's saying. The marks date from that day in the dungeon. I remember seeing the same lesions on the hand of the French writer I had been in another past life. It's called nummular eczema because the lesions are the same shape and size as a small Roman coin or *nummulus* – or a burn mark left by a red-hot coal.

The music stops. It's time we went to supper. I go over to Hilal and invite her partner to join us. He must be one of the readers chosen as guests for the night. Hilal looks at me in surprise.

'But you've already invited other people.'

'There's always room for one more,' I say.

'Not always. Not everything in life is a long train with tickets available to all.'

The young man doesn't quite understand this remark, but clearly senses that something odd is going on. He explains that he has promised to have supper with his family. I decide to have a little fun.

'Have you read Mayakovsky?' I ask.

'No. His work is not longer compulsory reading in schools. He was a kind of State poet.'

He's right, but I loved Mayakovsky's work when I was his age and I know a little about his life.

My publishers approach, fearful that I might be instigating a jealous brawl, but as so often in life, things are not what they seem.

'He fell in love with the wife of his publisher, a dancer,' I say teasingly. 'They had a passionate love affair and that was instrumental in making his poetry less political and more humane. Even though he always changed the names in his poems, the publisher knew perfectly well that Mayakovsky was writing about his wife, but continued publishing his books anyway. She loved her husband *and* Mayakovsky. The solution they found was for the three of them to live together, and very happy they were too.'

'Well, I love my husband *and* I love you!' jokes my publisher's wife. 'Why don't you move to Russia?'

The young man gets the message.

'Is she your girlfriend?' he asks.

'I've been in love with her for at least five hundred years, but the answer is no: she's as free as a bird. She's a young woman with a brilliant career ahead of her, but she hasn't yet met anyone who will treat her with the love and respect she deserves.'

'What rubbish. Do you really think I need someone to find me a husband?' says Hilal.

The young man explains again that he's expected at home for supper, then thanks us and leaves. The other invited readers join us and we set off to walk to the restaurant.

'Forgive me for saying this,' says Yao as we cross the road, 'but you acted quite wrongly just now as regards Hilal, the young man and yourself. With Hilal, because you failed to show due respect for the love she feels for you. With him, because he is one of your readers and felt he was being used. And with yourself, because you were motivated by pride and wanted to show him you were more important. It might have been forgivable if you had been acting out of jealousy, but you weren't. You were simply showing your friends and me that you didn't care, which isn't true.'

I nod in agreement. Spiritual growth doesn't always arrive hand-in-hand with wisdom.

'And another thing,' Yao goes on, 'Mayakovsky *was* compulsory reading at school, and, as everyone knows, that ménage à trois didn't end happily at all. Mayakovsky shot himself in the head when he was only thirty-seven.'

*   *   *

We are five hours ahead of Moscow time now. People there are just finishing lunch as we are starting our supper in Irkutsk. The city has its charm, but the atmosphere among us is tenser than it is on the train. Perhaps we've become used to our little world around the table, travelling towards a definite goal, and each stop means a diversion from our chosen path.

Hilal is in a particularly foul mood after what happened at the party. My publisher is arguing furiously with someone on his mobile phone, although Yao assures me that it's simply a discussion about distribution problems. The three invited readers seem even shyer than usual.

We order some drinks. One of the readers warns us to be careful because we're being served a mixture of Mongolian and Siberian vodka and will pay the price the next day if we over-indulge. However, we all need a drink in order to relieve the tension. We have one glass, then another, and before the food has even arrived, we've already ordered a second bottle. In the end, the reader who warned us about the vodka decides that he doesn't want to be the only sober person at the table and downs three glasses one after the other, while we applaud. Everyone cheers up, apart from Hilal, who remains resolutely glum despite drinking as much as the rest of us.

'This city's a dreadful place,' says the reader who had abstained from the vodka until two minutes ago and whose eyes are already bloodshot. 'You saw the street outside the restaurant.'

I had noticed a row of exquisite, wood-built houses, a rarity these days. It had struck me as being rather like an open-air architectural museum.

'I'm not talking about the houses, but about the street.'

True, the pavement wasn't the best I'd ever seen and here and there you did catch a whiff of sewers.

'You see, the mafia control this part of the city,' he goes on. 'They want to buy up the whole area and build another of their hideous housing developments. The residents have so far refused to sell their land and their houses, and so the mafia won't allow any improvements in the area. This city has been in existence for four hundred years, it received traders from China with open arms, and was respected by dealers in diamonds, gold and skins, but now the mafia is trying to move in and put a stop to all that, even though the government is fighting them ...'

'Mafia' is a universal word. My publisher is still busy with his interminable phone call, my editor is complaining about the menu, Hilal is pretending she's on another planet, while Yao and myself have suddenly noticed that a group of men on the next table have begun to take a close interest in our conversation.

Pure paranoia.

The reader continues drinking and complaining. His two friends agree with everything he says. They moan about the government, about the condition of the roads, the state of the airport. These are all things we would say about our own cities, except that here, every complaint includes the word 'mafia'. I try to change the subject and ask about the local shamans, which pleases Yao, who can see that even though I haven't yet said yes or no, his request has not been forgotten. But the young men start talking about the 'shaman mafia' and the 'tourist guide mafia'. A third bottle of Mongolian-Siberian vodka has arrived, and everyone is now excitedly discussing politics – in English so that I can understand or so that the people on the other tables can't. My publisher finally finishes his phone call and joins in the discussion, as, with equal gusto, does my editor, while Hilal downs one glass of vodka after another. Only Yao remains completely sober, apparently gazing off into the distance, trying to disguise his unease. I stopped after my third glass and have no intention of drinking more.

And what seemed like paranoia becomes a reality. One of the men at the other table gets up and comes over to us.

He doesn't say a word. He merely looks at the young men we invited to supper, and the conversation stops. Everyone seems surprised to see him there. My publisher, slightly befuddled by the vodka and by the distribution problem in Moscow, asks something in Russian.

'No, I'm not his father,' answers the stranger, 'but I don't know if he's old enough to drink like that and to say things that are completely untrue.'

His English is perfect, and he speaks with the rather affected accent of someone who has studied at one of the most expensive schools in England. His voice is cold and neutral, without a hint of emotion or aggression.

Only a fool makes threats, and only another fool feels threatened. When someone uses that tone, though, it spells danger, because subjects, verbs and predicates will, if necessary, be transformed into actions.

'You chose the wrong restaurant,' he says. 'The food here is terrible and the service even worse. Perhaps you'd better find somewhere else to eat. I'll pay the bill.'

The food really isn't very good, the drink is clearly as bad as we were warned it was, and the service is appalling. However, the man isn't concerned about our health and well-being: we are being thrown out.

'Let's go,' says the young reader.

Before we can do anything, he and his friends have vanished. The man seems pleased and turns to go back to his own table. For a fraction of a second, the tension dissolves.

'Well, I'm really enjoying the food and have no intention of going to another restaurant.'

Yao spoke in a voice equally devoid of emotion or menace. There was no need for him to say anything; the conflict was over; my readers had been the only ones causing the problem. We could simply have finished our meal in peace. The man turns to face him. One of his colleagues picks up his mobile phone and goes outside. The restaurant falls silent.

Yao and the stranger stare at each other.

'The food here can give you food poisoning and kill you almost instantly.'

Yao remains seated.

'According to statistics, in the three minutes that we've been talking, three hundred and twenty people in the world have died and another six hundred and fifty have been born. That's life. I don't know how many died of food poisoning, but some must have. Others died after a long illness, some suffered an accident, and probably a certain percentage got shot, while some poor woman died in childbirth and the unborn child became part of the birth statistics. Only the living die.'

The man who left the restaurant with his mobile phone has come back, and the stranger standing by our table continues to show no emotion. For what seems like an eternity, no one in the restaurant speaks. At last, the stranger says:

'Another minute has passed. Another hundred or so people must have died and another two hundred or so been born.'

'Exactly.'

Two more men appear at the door of the restaurant and walk over to our table. The stranger sees them and indicates with a jerk of his head that they should leave again.

'The food here may be terrible and the service appalling, but if this is the restaurant of your choice, I can do nothing about it. *Bon appétit.*'

'Thank you. But we'll gladly take you up on your offer to pay the bill.'

'Of course,' he says, addressing Yao only, as if no one else were there. He puts his hand in his pocket, and we all imagine that he's about to pull out a gun, but instead he produces an entirely unthreatening business card.

'Get in touch if you ever need a job or get tired of what you're doing now. Our property company has a large branch here in Russia and we need people like you, people who understand that death is just a statistic.'

He hands Yao his card, they shake hands, and he returns to his table. Gradually, the restaurant returns to life, the silence fills up with talk, and we gaze in astonishment at Yao, our hero, the man who defeated the enemy without firing a single shot. Hilal has cheered up too and is now trying to keep up with a ridiculous conversation in which everyone appears to have developed a sudden intense interest in stuffed birds and the quality of Mongolian-Siberian vodka. The adrenaline surge brought on by fear had an instantly sobering effect on us all.

I mustn't let this opportunity slip. I'll ask Yao later what made him so sure of himself. Now I say:

'You know, I'm very impressed by the religious faith of the Russian people. Communism spent seventy years telling them that religion was the opium of the people, but to no avail.'

'Marx clearly knew nothing about the marvels of opium,' says my editor, and everyone laughs. I go on:

'The same thing happened with the Church I belong to. We killed in God's name, we tortured in Jesus' name, we decided that women were a threat to society and so suppressed all displays of female ingenuity, we practised usury, murdered the innocent and made pacts with the Devil. And yet, two thousand years later, we're still here.'

'I hate churches,' says Hilal, taking the bait. 'My least enjoyable moment of this whole trip was when you forced me to go to that church in Novosibirsk.'

'Imagine that you believe in past lives and that, in one of your previous existences, you had been burned at the stake by the Inquisition in the name of the faith the Vatican was trying to impose. Would you hate the Church even more then?'

She barely hesitates before responding.

'No. It would still be a matter of indifference to me. Yao didn't hate the man who came over to our table; he simply prepared himself to do battle over a principle.'

'But what if you were innocent?'

My publisher interrupts. Perhaps he has brought out a book on this subject too …

'I'm reminded of Giordano Bruno. He was respected in the Church as a learned man, but was burned alive in the centre of Rome itself. During the trial, he said something along the lines of: "I am not afraid of the fire, but you are afraid of your verdict." A statue of him now stands in the place where he was murdered by his so-called "allies". He triumphed because he was judged by mere men, not by Jesus.'

'Are you trying to justify an injustice and a crime?'

'Not at all. The murderers vanished from the map, but Giordano Bruno continues to influence the world with his ideas. His courage was rewarded. After all, a life without a cause is a life without effect.'

It is as if the conversation were being guided in the direction I want it to go.

'If you were Giordano Bruno,' I say, looking directly at Hilal now, 'would you be able to forgive your executioners?'

'What are you getting at?'

'I belong to a religion that perpetrated horrors in the past. That's what I'm getting at, because, despite everything, I still have the love of Jesus, which is far stronger than the hatred of those who declared themselves to be his successors. And I still believe in the mystery of the transubstantiation of bread and wine.'

'That's your problem, but I just want to keep well away from churches, priests and sacraments. Music and the silent contemplation of nature are quite enough for me. But does what you're saying have something to do with what you saw when ...' She pauses to consider her words.'When you said you were going to do an exercise involving a ring of light?'

She doesn't say that we were in bed together. For all her strong character and hasty temperament, she is trying to protect me.

'I don't know. As I said on the train, everything that happened in the past or will happen in the future is also happening in the present. Perhaps we met because I was your executioner, you were my victim and it's time for me to ask your forgiveness.'

Everyone laughs and I do too.

'Well, be nicer to me then, be a little more attentive. Say to me now, in front of everyone, the three-word sentence I long to hear.'

I know that she wants me to say:'I love you.'

'I will say three three-word sentences: one, You are protected. Two, Do not worry. Three, I adore you.'

'Well, I have something to add to that. Only someone who can say "I love you" is capable of saying "I forgive you".'

Everyone applauds. We return to the Mongolian-Siberian vodka, and talk about love, persecution, crimes committed in the name of truth, and the food in the restaurant. The conversation will go no further tonight. She doesn't understand what I'm talking about, but the first, most difficult step has been taken.

As we leave, I ask Yao why he decided to take that line of action, thus putting everyone at risk.

'But nothing happened, did it?'

'No, but it could have. People like him aren't used to being treated with disrespect.'

'I was always getting kicked out of places when I was younger and I promised myself that it would never happen again once I was an adult. Besides, I didn't treat him with disrespect; I simply confronted him in the way he wanted to be confronted. The eyes don't lie, and he knew I wasn't bluffing.'

'Even so, you did challenge him. We're in a small city, and he could have felt that you were questioning his authority.'

'When we left Novosibirsk, you said something about that Aleph thing. A few days ago, I realised that the Chinese have a word for it too: *qi*. Both he and I were standing at the same energy point. I don't want to philosophise about what might have happened, but anyone accustomed to danger knows that, at any moment of his life, he could be confronted by an opponent – not an enemy, an opponent. When an opponent is sure of his power, as he was, you have to confront them or be undermined by your failure to exercise your own power. Knowing how to appreciate and honour our opponents is a far cry from what flatterers, wimps or traitors do.'

'But you know he was—'

'It doesn't matter what he was, what mattered was how he handled his energy. I liked his style of fighting, and he liked mine. That's all.'

The Golden Rose

I have a terrible headache after drinking all that Mongolian-Siberian vodka, and none of the pills and potions I've taken seem to help. It's a bright, cloudless day, but there's a biting wind. It may be late spring, but ice still mingles with the pebbles on the shore. Despite the various layers of clothing I've put on, the cold is unbearable.

But my one thought is: My God, I'm home!

Before me lies a vast lake, so big that I can barely see the farther shore. Against a backdrop of snow-capped mountains, a fishing-boat is setting out across the lake's transparent waters and will presumably return this evening. All I want is to be here, entirely present, because I don't know if I will ever come back. I take several deep breaths, trying to soak up the beauty of it all.

'It's one of the loveliest things I've ever seen.'

Encouraged by this remark, Yao decides to feed me some facts. He explains that Lake Baikal, called the North Sea in ancient Chinese texts, contains roughly 20 per cent of the world's surface fresh water and is more than twenty-five million years old. Unfortunately, none of this interests me.

'Don't distract me. I want to absorb this whole land-scape into my soul.'

'It's very big. Why don't you just plunge straight in and merge your soul with the soul of the lake?'

In other words, risk suffering thermal shock and dying of hypothermia in Siberia. He has finally managed to get my attention. My head is heavy, the wind unbear-able, and we decide to go straight to the place where we are to spend the night.

'Thank you for coming. You won't regret it.'

We go to an inn in a little village with dirt roads and houses like the ones I saw in Irkutsk. There is a well near the door, and a little girl is standing by the well, trying to draw up a bucket of water. Hilal goes to help her, but instead of pulling on the rope, she positions the child perilously near the edge.

'According to the *I Ching*,' I tell her, 'you can move a town, but you cannot move a well. I say that you can move the bucket, but not the child. Be careful.'

The child's mother comes over and berates Hilal. I leave them to it and go to my room. Yao had been vehe-mently opposed to Hilal coming with us. Women are not allowed in the place where we are going to meet the shaman. I told him that I wasn't particularly interested in making the visit. I know the Tradition, which is to be found everywhere, and I've met various shamans in my own country. I only agreed to go because Yao has helped me and taught me many things during the journey.

'I need to spend every second I can with Hilal,' I said while we were still in Irkutsk. 'I know what I'm doing. I am on the path back to my kingdom. If she doesn't help me now, I will have only three more chances in this "life".'

He didn't understand exactly what I meant, but he gave in.

I put my backpack down in one corner of my room, turn the heating up to maximum, close the curtains and fall onto the bed, hoping my headache will go away. At this point, Hilal comes in.

'You left me out there talking to that woman. You know I hate strangers.'

'We're the strangers here.'

'I hate being judged all the time and having to hide my fear, my emotions, my vulnerabilities. You think I'm a brave, talented young woman, who is never intimidated by anything. Well, you're wrong. Everything intimidates me. I avoid glances, smiles, close contact. You're the only person I've really talked to. Or haven't you noticed?'

Lake Baikal, snow-capped mountains, limpid water, one of the most beautiful places on the planet, and this stupid conversation.

'Let's rest for a while, then we can go out for a walk. I'm meeting the shaman tonight.'

She makes as if to put down her backpack, but I say:

'You have your own room.'

'But on the train …'

228

Aleph

She doesn't complete her sentence, and leaves, slamming the door. I lie there staring up at the ceiling, wondering what to do. I can't let myself be guided by my feelings of guilt. I can't and I won't, because I love another woman who is far away just now and who trusts her husband, even though she knows him well. All my previous attempts at explanation have failed; perhaps here would be the ideal place to set things straight once and for all with this obsessive, adaptable, strong, but fragile young woman.

I am not to blame for what is happening. Neither is Hilal. Life has placed us in this situation, and I just hope it is for the good of both of us. Hope? I'm sure it is. I start praying and immediately fall asleep.

When I wake up, I go to her room and, from outside, can hear her playing the violin. I wait until she has finished, then knock on the door.

'Let's go for a walk.'

She looks at me, surprised and happy.

'Are you feeling better? Can you stand the wind and the cold?'

'Yes, I'm much better. Let's go.'

We walk through the village, which is like somewhere out of a fairy tale. One day, tourists will come here, vast hotels will be built, shops will sell T-shirts, lighters, postcards, models of the wooden houses. They will make huge car parks for the double-decker coaches bringing people armed with digital cameras, determined to capture the whole lake on a microchip. The well we saw will be destroyed and replaced by another, more decorative one; however, it won't supply the inhabitants with water, but will be sealed up by order of the council, so that no foreign children risk leaning over the edge and falling in. The fishing-boat I saw this morning will vanish. The waters of the lake will be criss-crossed by modern yachts offering day cruises to the centre of the lake, lunch included. Professional fishermen and hunters will arrive, armed with the necessary licences, for which they will pay, per day, the equivalent of what the local fishermen and hunters earn in a year.

Aleph

At the moment, though, it's just a remote village in Siberia, where a man and a woman half his age are walking alongside a river created by the thaw. They sit down beside it.

'Do you remember our conversation last night in the restaurant?'

'More or less. I had rather a lot to drink, but I remember Yao standing up to that Englishman.'

'I talked about the past.'

'Yes, I remember. I understood perfectly what you said, because during that moment when we were in the Aleph, I saw that your eyes were full of a mixture of love and indifference, and your head was covered by a hood. I felt betrayed and humiliated. But I'm not interested in what our relationship was in a past life. We're here in the present.'

'You see this river? Well, in the living room in my apartment at home is a painting of a rose immersed in just such a river. Half of the painting was exposed to the effects of the water and the elements, so the edges are a bit rough, and yet I can still see part of that beautiful red rose against a gold background. I know the artist. In 2003, we went together to a forest in the Pyrenees and found a dried-up stream and we hid the painting under the stones on the stream bed.

'The artist is my wife. At this moment, she's thousands of kilometres away and will still be sleeping because day has not yet dawned in her city, although here it's four o'clock in the afternoon. We've been together for more than a quarter of a century. When I met her, I was convinced that our relationship wouldn't work out, and for the first two years, I was sure that one of us would leave. In the five years that followed, I continued to think that we had simply got used to one another and that as soon as we realised this, we would each go our separate ways. I thought that a more serious commitment would deprive me of my "liberty" and keep me from experiencing everything I wanted to experience.'

I see that Hilal is starting to feel uncomfortable.

'And what has that got to do with the river and the rose?'

'By the summer of 2002, I was already a well-known writer with plenty of money and I believed that my basic values hadn't changed. But how could I be sure? I decided to test things out. We rented a small room in a two-star hotel in France, intending to spend five months of the year there. There was just one small wardrobe in the room and so we had to keep clothes to the minimum. We went for long walks in the forests and the mountains, ate out, spent hours talking, and went to the cinema every day. Living like that confirmed to us that the most sophisticated things in the world are precisely those within the reach of everyone.

'We both love what we do, but whereas all I need is a laptop, my wife is a painter, and painters need vast studios in which to produce and store their paintings. I didn't want her to give up her vocation for my sake, and so I suggested renting a studio. Meanwhile, though, she had looked around her at the mountains, valleys, rivers, lakes and forests and thought: Why don't I store my paintings here? Why don't I let nature work with me?'

Hilal's eyes are fixed on the river.

'That was where she got the idea of "storing" pictures in the open air. I would take my laptop and do my writing, while she knelt on the grass and painted. A year later, when we went back for the first canvases, the results were quite extraordinary and totally original. The first painting we "unearthed" was the one of the rose. Nowadays, even though we have a house in the Pyrenees, she continues to inter and disinter her paintings wherever she happens to be. Something that was born out of necessity has become her main creative method. When I look at this river, I remember that rose and feel an almost palpable, physical love for her, as if she were here.'

The wind isn't blowing quite as hard now, and the sun warms us a little. The light surrounding us could not be more perfect.

'I understand and respect what you're saying,' she says. 'But in the restaurant, when you were talking about the past, you said something about love being stronger than the individual.'

'Yes, but love is made up of choices.'

'In Novosibirsk, you made me forgive you and I did. Now I'm asking you a favour: tell me that you love me.'

I take her hand. We are both gazing at the river.

'Silence is also an answer,' she says.

I put my arms around her, so that her head is resting on my shoulder.

'I love you,' I tell her, 'I love you because all the loves in the world are like different rivers flowing into the same lake, where they meet and are transformed into a single love that becomes rain and blesses the earth.

'I love you like a river that creates the right conditions for trees and bushes and flowers to flourish along its banks. I love you like a river that gives water to the thirsty and takes people where they want to go.

'I love you like a river which understands that it must learn to flow differently over waterfalls and to rest in the shallows. I love you because we are all born in the same place, at the same source, which keeps us provided with a constant supply of water. And so, when we feel weak, all we have to do is wait a little. The spring returns, the winter snows melt and fill us with new energy.

'I love you like a river that begins as a solitary trickle in the mountains and gradually grows and joins other rivers until, after a certain point, it can flow around any obstacle in order to get where it wants.

'I receive your love and I give you mine. Not the love of a man for a woman, not the love of a father for a child, not the love of God for his creatures, but a love with no name and no explanation, like a river that cannot explain why it follows a particular course, but simply flows onwards. A love that asks for nothing and gives nothing in return; it is simply there. I will never be yours and you will never be mine; nevertheless, I can honestly say: I love you, I love you, I love you.'

Maybe it's the afternoon, maybe it's the light, but at that moment, the Universe seems finally to be in perfect harmony. We stay where we are, feeling not the slightest desire to go back to the hotel, where Yao will doubtless be waiting for me.

The Eagle of Baikal

Any moment now, it will be dark. There are six of us standing near a small boat moored at the lake shore: Hilal, Yao, the shaman, myself and two older women. They are all speaking in Russian. The shaman is shaking his head. Yao appears to be arguing with him, but the shaman turns away and walks over to the boat.

Now Yao and Hilal are arguing. He seems concerned, but I think he's rather enjoying the situation. We have been practising the Path of Peace together, and I can interpret his body language now. He is pretending an irritation that he doesn't actually feel.

'What are you talking about?' I ask.

'Apparently, I can't go with you,' Hilal says. 'I have to stay with these two women whom I've never seen in my life and spend the whole night here in the cold, because there's no one to take me back to the hotel.'

'You will experience with them whatever we experience on the island,' Yao explains. 'But we cannot break with tradition. I warned you before, but he insisted on bringing you. We have to leave now because we cannot

236

miss the moment, or what you call the Aleph and I call *qi*, and for which the shamans doubtless have their own word. It won't take long. We'll be back in a couple of hours.'

'Come on,' I say, taking Yao by the arm, but first turning to Hilal with a smile. 'You wouldn't have wanted to stay at the hotel, knowing that you might miss out on some new experience. I don't know whether it will be good or bad, but it's better than having supper alone.'

'And you, I suppose, think that fine words of love are enough to feed a heart? I know you love your wife, and I understand that, but couldn't you at least give me some reward for all the universes I'm placing at your door?'

I turn away. Another idiotic conversation.

The shaman starts the engine and takes the rudder. We are heading for what looks like a rock about two hundred metres from the shore. I reckon it will take us only a few minutes to get there.

'Now that there's no turning back, why were you so insistent that I should meet this shaman? It's the only favour you've asked of me on the entire trip, and you've given me so much. I don't just mean the aikido practice. You've helped keep harmony on the train, you've translated my words as if they were yours and yesterday you demonstrated the importance of going into battle simply out of respect for your opponent.'

Yao shakes his head and looks rather uncomfortable, as if he were entirely responsible for the safety of the little boat.

'I just thought, given your interests, that you'd like to meet him.'

This is not a good reply. If I had wanted to meet the shaman, I would have asked. Finally, he looks at me and nods.

'I asked you because I made a promise to come back on my next trip here. I could have come on my own, but I signed a contract with your publishers, guaranteeing that I would always be by your side. They wouldn't like it if I left you alone.'

'I don't always need people around me, and my publishers wouldn't have been bothered if you had left me in Irkutsk.'

Night is falling faster than I expected. Yao changes the subject.

'The man steering the boat has the ability to speak to my wife. I know he's not lying because there are certain things no one else could possibly know. More than that, he saved my daughter. He did what no doctor in the finest hospitals in Moscow, Beijing, Shanghai or London could do. And he asked for nothing in return, only that I come to see him again. It's just that this time I'm with you. Maybe I'll finally learn to understand the things that my brain refuses to accept.'

We are getting closer to the rock now. We should be there in less than a minute.

'That is a good answer. Thank you for trusting me. I am in one of the most beautiful places in the world, on an exquisite evening, listening to the waves lapping against the boat. Going to meet this man is just one of the many blessings I have received on this trip.'

Except for the day when he spoke to me of his grief at losing his wife, Yao has never shown any emotion. Now he takes my hand and presses it to his chest. The boat runs ashore on a narrow strip of pebbles, which serves as anchor.

'Thank you. Thank you very much.'

We climb up to the top of the rock, in time to catch a last glimpse of red sky on the horizon. There is nothing but scrub around us, and to the east stand three or four bare trees that have not yet put out their leaves. On one of them are the remains of offerings and the carcass of an animal hanging from a branch. I feel great respect for the old shaman's wisdom, but he won't show me anything new, because I have already walked many paths and know that they all lead to the same place. Nevertheless, I can see that he is serious in his intentions, and while he prepares the ritual, I try to remember all I have learned about the role of the shaman in the history of civilisation.

*   *   *

In ancient times, there were always two dominant figures in a tribe. The first was the leader. He would be the bravest member of the tribe, strong enough to defeat any challengers and intelligent enough to foil any conspiracies – power struggles are nothing new, they have been with us since the dawn of time. Once he was established in his position, he became responsible for the protection and well-being of his people in the physical world. With time, what had been a matter of natural selection became subject to corruption, and leadership began to be passed down from father to son, giving way to the principle of perpetuation of power, from which emperors, kings and dictators spring.

More important than the leader, however, was the shaman. Even at the very dawn of humanity, men were already aware of some greater power, capable both of giving life and taking it away, although where exactly that power came from they didn't know. Along with the birth of love came a need to find an answer to the mystery of existence. The first shamans were women, the source of life. Since they did not have to go hunting or fishing, they could devote themselves to contemplation and immerse themselves in the sacred mysteries. The Tradition was always passed on to those who were most able, who lived alone and isolated and were usually virgins. They worked on a different plane, balancing the forces of the spiritual world with those of the physical world.

The process was nearly always the same: the shaman used music (usually percussion) to go into a trance, and then would drink and administer potions made from natural substances. Her soul would leave her body and enter the parallel universe. There it would meet with the spirits of plants, animals, the dead and the living, all existing in a single time, what Yao calls *qi* and I call the Aleph. There, too, she would encounter her guides, and be able to balance energies, cure illnesses, bring rain, restore peace, decipher the symbols and signs sent by nature, and punish any individual who was getting in the way of the tribe's contact with the All. At that time, when tribes had to keep travelling in their constant search for food, it was impossible to build temples or altars. There was only the All, in whose womb the tribe journeyed ever onward.

Like the role of leader, that of shaman also became corrupted. Since the health and protection of the group depended on being in harmony with the forest, the countryside and nature, the women responsible for that spiritual contact – the soul of the tribe – were invested with great authority, often more even than the leader. At some undefined moment in history (probably after the discovery of agriculture, which brought an end to nomadism), the female gift was usurped by men. Force won out over harmony. The natural qualities of those women were ignored; what mattered was their power.

The next step was to organise shamanism – now entirely male – into a social structure. The first religions came into being. Society had changed and was no longer nomadic, but respect for and fear of the leader and the shaman were rooted in the human soul and would remain so for ever. Aware of this, the priests joined ranks with the tribal leaders in order to keep the people in submission. Anyone who defied the governors would be threatened with punishment by the gods. Then came a time when women started demanding back their role as shamans, because without them the world was heading for conflict. Whenever they put themselves forward, however, they were treated as heretics and prostitutes. If the system felt threatened by them, it did not hesitate to punish them with burnings, stonings and, in milder instances, exile. Female religions were erased from the history of civilisation; we know only that the most ancient magical objects so far uncovered by archaeologists are images of goddesses. They, however, were lost in the sands of time, just as magical powers, when used only for earthly ends, became diluted and lost their potency. All that remained was the fear of divine punishment.

efore me now stands a man, not a woman, although the women who stayed behind on the lake shore with Hilal doubtless have the same powers. I don't question his presence here, for both sexes possess the gift that will allow them to enter into contact with the unknown, as long as they are open to their 'feminine side'. What lies behind my lack of enthusiasm for this meeting is knowing just how far humanity has drifted from its origins and contact with the Dream of God.

The shaman is lighting a fire in a hollow dug in the ground to protect the flames from the wind that continues to blow. He places a kind of drum next to the fire and opens a bottle containing some unfamiliar liquid. The shaman in Siberia – where the term originated – is following the same rituals as the *pajé* in the Amazonian jungle, as *hechiceros* in Mexico, *candomblé* priests from Africa, spiritualists in France, *curanderos* in indigenous American tribes, Aborigines in Australia, charismatics in the Catholic Church, Mormons in Utah, etc. etc.

That is what is so surprising about these traditions, which seem to live in eternal conflict with each other. They meet on the same spiritual plane and are to be found all over the world, even though they have nothing to do with each other on the physical plane. That is the Great Mother saying:

243

'Sometimes, my children have eyes, but cannot see, ears, but cannot hear. I will therefore demand that some should not be deaf and blind to me. They may have to pay a high price, but they will be responsible for keeping the Tradition alive, and one day, My blessings will return to the Earth.'

The shaman begins beating on the drum, gradually getting faster and faster. He says something to Yao, who immediately translates:

'He didn't use the word *qi*, but he says the *qi* will come on the wind.'

The wind is getting stronger. Even though I am well wrapped up – special anorak, gloves, thick woollen hat and a scarf up to my eyes – it's not enough. My nose appears to have lost all feeling, small ice crystals gather on my eyebrows and beard. Yao is kneeling, his legs folded neatly beneath him. I try to do the same, but have to keep changing position because I'm wearing ordinary trousers and the chill wind penetrates them, numbing my muscles and causing painful cramps.

The flames dance wildly about, but do not go out. The drumming grows more furious. The shaman is trying to make his heart keep time with the beating of his hand on the leather skin, the bottom part of the drum being left open to let in the spirits. In the Afro-Brazilian tradition, this is the moment when the medium or priest lets his soul leave his body, allowing another more experienced being to occupy it. The only difference is that in my country there is no precise moment for what Yao calls *qi* to manifest itself.

I cease being a mere observer and decide to join in the trance. I try to make my heart keep time with the beats; I close my eyes, empty my mind, but the cold and the wind won't allow me to go further than that. I need to change position again; I open my eyes and notice that the shaman is holding a few feathers in one hand – possibly from some rare local bird. According to traditions throughout the world, birds are the messengers of the gods. They help the shaman rise up and speak with the spirits.

Yao has his eyes open too; only the shaman will enter that ecstatic state. The wind increases in intensity. I am feeling colder and colder, but the shaman appears utterly impervious. The ritual continues. He takes the bottle containing a greenish liquid, drinks and hands the bottle to Yao, who also drinks before handing it to me. Out of respect, I follow suit and take a mouthful of the sugary, slightly alcoholic mixture, then return the bottle to the shaman.

The drumming continues, interrupted only when the shaman pauses to trace a shape on the ground, symbols I have never seen before and which resemble some long since vanished form of writing. Strange noises emerge from his throat, like the greatly amplified cries of birds. The drumming is getting louder and faster all the time;

the cold doesn't seem to bother me much now and, suddenly, the wind stops.

I need no explanations. What Yao calls *qi* is here. The three of us look at each other, and a kind of calm descends. The person before me is not the same man who steered the boat or who asked Hilal to stay behind on the shore; his features have changed, and he looks younger, more feminine.

He and Yao talk in Russian for a while, how long I can't say. The horizon brightens. The moon is rising. I accompany it on its new journey across the sky, its silvery rays reflected in the waters of the lake, which, from one moment to the next, have grown utterly still. To my left, the lights of the village come on. I feel utterly serene, trying to take in as much of this unexpected moment as I can, because I had not expected this; it was simply lying in my path, along with many other unexpected moments. If only the unexpected always wore this pretty, peaceful face.

Finally, through Yao, the shaman asks me why I am here.

'To be with my friend who had made a promise to return here. To honour your art. And to share with you in the contemplation of the mystery.'

'The man beside you does not believe in anything,' says the shaman through Yao. 'He has come here several times in order to speak to his wife, and yet he still does not believe. Poor woman! Instead of walking with God while she awaits her time to return to Earth, she has to keep coming back to console this poor unfortunate. She leaves the warmth of the divine Sun for this wretched Siberian cold because love will not let her go!'

The shaman laughs.

'Why don't you tell him?'

'I have, but he, like most people I know, won't accept what he considers to be a loss.'

'Pure selfishness.'

'Yes, pure selfishness. People like him would like time to stop or go backwards, and by doing so, they prevent the souls of their loved ones from moving on.'

The shaman laughs again.

'When his wife passed on to another plane, he killed God, and he will keep coming back once, twice, ten times, to try again and again to talk to her. He doesn't ask for help in order to understand life better. He wants things to conform to his way of seeing life and death.'

He pauses and looks around him. It is now completely dark, apart from the light from the flames.

'I cannot cure despair when people find comfort in it.'

'Who am I talking to?'

'You are a believer.'

I repeat the question, and he answers:

'Valentina.'

A woman.

'The man at my side may be slightly foolish when it comes to things spiritual, but he is an excellent human being, prepared for anything except what he calls the "death" of his wife. The man at my side is a good man.'

The shaman nods.

'So are you. You came with a friend who has been by your side for a long time, long before you met in this life. As have I.'

Another laugh.

'It was in a different place and we met the same fate in battle, what your friend here calls "death". I don't know in which country it was, but the wounds were caused by bullets. Warriors meet again. It is part of the divine law.'

He throws some herbs onto the flames, explaining that we have done this too in another life, sitting around a fire and talking about our adventures.

'Your spirit converses with the eagle of Baikal, which watches over and guards everything, attacking enemies and protecting and defending friends.'

As if to confirm his words, we hear a bird far off. The feeling of cold has been replaced by one of well-being. He again holds out the bottle to us.

'Fermented drinks are alive; they pass from youth to old age. When they reach maturity, they can destroy the Spirit of Inhibition, the Spirit of Loneliness, the Spirit of Fear, the Spirit of Anxiety. But if you drink too much of them, they rebel and usher in the Spirit of Defeat and Aggression. It's all a matter of knowing when to stop.'

We drink and celebrate.

'At this moment, your body is on the earth, but your spirit is with me up here in the heights, and that is all I can offer you, a stroll through the skies above Baikal. You did not come here to ask for anything, and so I will give you only that. I hope it will inspire you to continue doing what you do.

'Be blessed. And just as you are transforming your own life, may you transform the lives of those around you. When they ask, do not forget to give. When they knock at your door, be sure to open it. When they lose something and come to you, do whatever you can to help them find what they have lost. First, though, ask, knock at the door and find out what is missing from your life. A hunter always knows what to expect – eat or be eaten.'

I nod.

'You have experienced this before and will do so many times,' the shaman goes on. 'Someone who is your friend is also a friend of the eagle of Baikal. Nothing special will happen tonight; you will have no visions, no magical experiences or trances that bring you into contact with the living or the dead. You will receive no special power. You will merely feel joy when the eagle of Baikal shows the lake to your soul. You will see nothing, but up above, your spirit will be filled with delight.'

My spirit is indeed filled with delight, even though I can see nothing. I don't have to. I know he is telling the truth. When my spirit returns to my body, it will be wiser and calmer.

Time stops, because I can no longer keep track of it. The flames flicker, casting strange shadows on the shaman's face, but I am barely here. I allow my spirit to go strolling; it needs to, after so much work and effort by my side. I don't feel cold any more. I don't feel anything. I am free and will remain so for as long as the eagle of Baikal is flying over the lake and the snowy mountains. It's a shame that my spirit cannot tell me what it sees, but then again, I don't need to know everything that happens to me.

The wind is getting up again. The shaman makes a low bow to the earth and to the sky. The fire, in the shelter of its hole, suddenly goes out. I look at the moon, which is high in the sky now, and I can see the shapes of birds flying around us. The shaman is once again an old man. He seems tired as he puts his drum back into a large embroidered bag.

Yao sticks his hand in his left pocket and pulls out a handful of coins and notes. I do the same. Yao says:

'We went begging for the eagle of Baikal. Here is what we received.'

The shaman bows, thanks us for the money, and we all walk unhurriedly back to the boat. The sacred island of the shamans has its own spirit; it is dark and we can never be sure that we are putting our feet in the right place.

When we reach the shore we look for Hilal, but the two women explain that she has gone back to the hotel. Only then do I realise that the shaman did not mention her once.

Fear of Fear

The heating in my room is on maximum. Before even bothering to reach for the light switch, I take off my anorak, hat and scarf and go over to the window, intending to open it and let in a little fresh air. The hotel is on a small hill, and I can see the lights of the village below going out one by one. I stand there for a while, imagining the marvels that my spirit must have seen. Then, just as I'm about to turn round, I hear a voice say:

'Don't turn round.'

Hilal is there, and the tone in which she says these words frightens me. She sounds deadly serious.

'I'm armed.'

No, that's impossible. Unless those women …

'Take a few steps back.'

I do as ordered.

'A little more. That's it. Now take a step to the right. OK, stop there.'

I'm not thinking any more, the survival instinct has taken charge of all my reactions. In a matter of seconds, my mind has processed what my options are: I could throw myself on the floor or try to strike up a conversation or simply wait and see what she does next. If she really is determined to kill me, she'll do so soon, but if she doesn't shoot in the next few minutes, she'll start talking and that will improve my chances.

There is a deafening noise, an explosion, and I find myself covered in shards of glass. The bulb above my head has burst.

'In my right hand I have my bow and in my left my violin. No, don't turn round.'

I stay where I am and breathe a sigh of relief. There's nothing magical or special about what has just happened: opera singers can shatter a champagne glass, for example, by singing a particular note that makes the air vibrate at a frequency that can cause very fragile objects to break.

The bow touches the strings again, producing the same piercing sound.

'I know what happened. I saw it. The women took me there with no need for a ring of light.'

She's seen it.

An immense weight is lifted off my glass-strewn shoulders. Yao doesn't know it, but our journey to this place is also part of my journey back to my kingdom. I didn't need to tell her anything. She had seen it.

'You abandoned me when I most needed you. I died because of you and have returned now to haunt you.'

'You're not haunting me or frightening me. I was forgiven.'

'You forced me to forgive you. I didn't know what I was doing.'

Another shrill, unpleasant chord.

'If you like, you can withdraw your forgiveness.'

'No, I don't want to. You *are* forgiven. And if you needed me to forgive you a hundred times over, I would. But the images were very confused in my mind. I need you to tell me exactly what happened. I remember only that I was naked. You were looking at me, and I was telling everyone there that I loved you and that was why I was condemned to death. My love condemned me.'

'Can I turn round now?'

'Not yet. First, tell me what happened. All I know is that in a past life, I died because of you. It could have been here, it could have been somewhere else in the world, but I sacrificed myself in the name of love, to save you.'

My eyes have grown accustomed to the darkness now, but the heat in the room is unbearable.

'What did those women do exactly?'

'We sat down together on the lake shore; they lit a fire, beat on a drum, went into a trance and gave me something to drink. When I drank, I started getting these confusing images in my head. They didn't last long. All I remember is what I've just told you. I thought it was some kind of nightmare, but they assured me that you and I had been together in a past life. You told me so yourself.'

Aleph

'No, it happened in the present; it's happening now. At this moment, I'm in a hotel room in Siberia, in some nameless village, but I'm also in a dungeon near Córdoba in Spain. I'm with my wife in Brazil, as well as with the many other women I've known, and in some of those lives, I myself am a woman. Play something.'

I take off my sweater. She starts to play a sonata not originally written for the violin. My mother used to play it on the piano when I was a child.

'There was a time when the world, too, was a woman, and her energy was very beautiful. People believed in miracles, the present moment was all there was and so time did not exist. The Greeks have two words for time, the first of which is *kairos*, meaning God's time, eternity. Then a change occurred. The battle for survival, the need to know when to plant crops so that they could be harvested. That was when time as we know it now became part of our history. The Greeks call it *chronos*; the Romans called it Saturn, a god whose first act was to devour his own children. We became the slaves of memory. Keep playing and I'll explain more clearly.'

She continues to play. I start to cry, but manage to keep talking.

'At this moment, I am in a garden in a town, sitting on a bench at the back of my house, looking up at the sky and trying to work out what people mean when they use the expression "building castles in the air", an expression I first heard an hour ago. I am seven years

255

old. I am trying to build a golden castle, but finding it hard to concentrate. My friends are having supper in their houses; my mother is playing the same music I'm hearing now, only on the piano. If I didn't feel the need to describe what I'm feeling, I would be entirely there. The smell of summer, cicadas singing in the trees, and me thinking about the little girl I'm in love with.

'I'm not in the past, I'm in the present. I am the little boy I was then. I will always be that little boy, we will all be the children, grown-ups, old people we were and will become. I am not *remembering*, I am *re-living* that time.'

I can't go on. I cover my face with my hands and weep, while she plays ever more intensely, ever more exquisitely, transporting me back to the many people I am and was. I am not crying for my dead mother, because she is here now, playing for me. I am not crying for the child who, puzzled by a strange turn of phrase, is trying to build a golden castle that keeps disappearing. That child is here as well, listening to Chopin; he knows how lovely the music is, having listened to it often, and would happily hear it again and again. I am crying because there is no other way of showing what I feel: I AM ALIVE. I am alive in every pore and every cell of my body. I am alive. I was never born and never died.

I may have my moments of sadness or confusion, but above me is the great I, who understands everything and laughs at my sufferings. I am crying for what is ephemeral and eternal, because I know that words are much poorer than music, and so I will never be able to describe this moment. I let Chopin, Beethoven and Wagner lead me into that past which is also the present, for their music is far more powerful than any golden ring.

I cry while Hilal plays, and she plays until I grow tired of crying.

She walks over to the light switch. The shattered bulb short-circuits. The room remains in darkness. She goes to the bedside table and switches on the lamp.

'Now you can turn round.'

When my eyes get used to the brightness, I see that she is completely naked, her arms spread wide, her bow and violin in her hands.

'Today you said that you loved me like a river. I want to tell you now that I love you like the music of Chopin. Simple and profound, as blue as the lake, capable of—'

'The music speaks for itself. There's no need to say anything.'

'I'm afraid, very afraid. What was it I saw exactly?'

I describe in detail everything that happened in the dungeon, my own cowardice and the girl who looked then exactly as she does now, except that her hands were bound with lengths of rope, a far cry from the strings on her bow or violin. She listens in silence, her arms still spread wide, absorbing my every word. We are both standing in the middle of the room; her body is as

257

white as that of the fifteen-year-old girl now being led to a pyre built near the city of Córdoba. I will not be able to save her, and I know that she will vanish into the flames along with her friends. This happened once and is happening over and over again, and will continue to happen as long as the world exists. I mention to her that the girl had pubic hair, whereas she has shaved hers off, something I hate, as if all men were looking for a child to have sex with. I ask her not to do that again, and she promises she won't.

I show her the patches of eczema on my skin which seem angrier and more visible than usual. I explain that they are the marks from that same place and past. I ask if she remembers what she said, or what the other girls said, while they were being led to the pyre. She shakes her head and asks:

'Do you desire me?'

'Yes, I do. We're here alone in this unique place on the planet. You are standing naked before me. I desire you very much.'

'I'm afraid of my fear. I'm asking myself for forgiveness, not for being here but because I have always been selfish in my pain. Instead of forgiving, I sought vengeance. Not because I was the stronger party, but because I always felt myself to be the weaker one. Whenever I hurt other people, I was only hurting myself even more. I humiliated others in order to feel humiliated, I attacked others in order to feel that my own feelings were being violated.

'I know I'm not the only person to have been through what I described that night at the embassy, being abused by a neighbour and friend of the family. I said then that it wasn't a rare experience, and I'm sure that at least one of the women there had been sexually abused as a child. But not everyone behaves as I have. I'm simply not at peace with myself.'

She takes a deep breath, trying to find the right words, then goes on:

'I can't get over what everyone else seems perfectly able to get over. You are in search of your treasure, and I am part of it. Nevertheless, I feel like a stranger in my own skin. The only reason I don't throw myself into your arms, kiss you and make love with you now is that I lack the courage and am afraid of losing you. While you were setting out in search of your kingdom, I was beginning to find myself, until, at a certain point on the journey, I couldn't go any further. That was when I started to get more aggressive. I feel rejected, useless, and there's nothing you can say that will make me change my mind.'

I sit down on the one chair in the room and ask her to sit on my lap. Her body is damp with sweat because of the excessive heat. She keeps hold of her violin and bow.

'I'm afraid of lots of things,' I say, 'and always will be. I'm not going to try and explain anything, but there is something you could do right now.'

'I don't want to go on telling myself that one day it will pass. It won't. I have to learn to live with my demons.'

'Wait. I didn't make this journey in order to save the world, far less to save you, but according to the magical Tradition, it's possible to transfer pain. It won't disappear instantly, but it will gradually disappear as you transfer it to another place. You've been doing this unconsciously all your life. Now I suggest you do it consciously.'

'Don't you want to make love with me?'

'Very much. At this moment, even though the room is boiling hot, I'm generating even more heat at the spot where your body is in contact with my legs. I'm no Superman. That's why I'm asking you to transfer both your pain and my desire. I want you to get up, go to your room and play your violin until you're exhausted. We're the only guests in the hotel, so no one is going to complain about the noise. Pour all your feelings into your music and do the same again tomorrow. Whenever you play, tell yourself that the thing that hurt you so much has become a gift. You're wrong when you say that other people have recovered from the trauma, they've simply hidden it away in a place they never go to. In your case, though, God has shown you the way. The power of regeneration is in your hands.'

'I love you as I love Chopin. I always wanted to be a pianist, but the violin was all my parents could afford at the time.'

'And I love you like a river.'

She gets up and starts to play. The heavens hear the music, and the angels come down to join me in listening to that naked woman who sometimes stands still and sometimes sways her body in time to the music and the violin. I desired her and made love with her, without ever touching her or having an orgasm. Not because I'm the most faithful man in the world, but because that was the way in which our bodies met – with the angels watching over us.

For the third time that night – the first was when my spirit flew with the eagle of Baikal, the second when I heard that childhood tune – time had stopped. I was entirely there, with no past or future, experiencing the music with her, that unexpected prayer, and feeling grateful that I had set off in search of my kingdom. I lay down on the bed, and she continued to play. I fell asleep to the sound of her violin.

I woke at first light, went to her room and saw her face. For the first time, she looked like an ordinary twenty-one-year-old woman. I woke her gently and asked her to get dressed because Yao was waiting for us to have breakfast. We had to get back to Irkutsk. The train would be leaving in a few hours.

We go downstairs, eat some marinated fish for breakfast (the only thing on the menu at that hour), then we hear the sound of the car that has come to fetch us drawing up outside. The driver greets us, picks up our bags and puts them in the boot.

We emerge from the hotel into brilliant sunshine, clear skies and no wind. The snowy mountains in the distance are clearly visible. I pause to say goodbye to the lake, knowing that I will probably never be back. Yao and Hilal get into the car, and the driver starts the engine.

But I can't move.

'We'd better go. I've allowed an extra hour, just in case there's some accident en route, but I don't want to risk missing the train.'

The lake is calling to me.

Yao gets out of the car and comes over to me.

'You were perhaps expecting more from that meeting last night with the shaman, but it was very important to me.'

I had, in fact, expected less. Later I will tell him what happened with Hilal. Now I am looking at the lake, which is dawning along with the sun, its waters reflecting every ray. My spirit had visited it with the eagle of Baikal, but I need to know it better.

'Things aren't always the way we expect them to be,' he goes on. 'But I'm really grateful to you for coming.'

'Is it possible to deviate from the path God has made? Yes, but it's always a mistake. Is it possible to avoid pain? Yes, but you'll never learn anything. Is it possible to know something without ever having experienced it? Yes, but it will never truly be part of you.'

And with those words, I walk towards the waters that continue to call to me. I do so slowly at first, hesitantly, unsure as to whether I will reach them. When I feel reason trying to hold me back, I start to walk more quickly, then break into a run, pulling off my winter clothes as I do. By the time I reach the edge of the lake, I am wearing only my underpants. For a moment, a fraction of a second, I hesitate, but my doubts are not strong enough to prevent me going forward. The icy water touches first my feet, then my ankles. The bottom of the lake is covered in stones and I have difficulty maintaining my balance, but I keep going, until the water is deep enough to – DIVE IN!

My body enters the freezing water, I feel thousands of needles pricking my skin, I stay under for as long as I can, a few seconds perhaps, perhaps an eternity, then I return to the surface.

Summer! Heat!

Later, I realise that anyone moving from a very cold place to a warmer place experiences the same sensation. There I was, with no shirt on, knee-deep in the waters of Lake Baikal, as happy as a child, because I had been enfolded in an energy that was now part of me.

Yao and Hilal had followed me and were watching incredulously from the shore.

'Come on! Come on in!'

They both start getting undressed. Hilal has nothing on underneath and is once again completely naked. But what does that matter? Some people gather on the pier and watch us. But, again, who cares? The lake is ours. The world is ours.

Yao is first in. He doesn't realise how uneven the bottom of the lake is and falls. He gets up, wades in a little further, then takes the plunge. Hilal must have levitated over the pebbles, because she enters at a run, going further out than either of us before plunging deep in; then she opens her arms to the skies and laughs like a loon.

No more than five minutes could have passed from the moment when I started running towards the lake until the moment we emerged. The driver, beside himself with worry, comes running towards us, bearing towels hastily borrowed from the hotel. We are leaping gleefully up and down, hugging each other, singing, shouting and saying: 'It's so hot out here!' – like the children we will never ever cease to be.

The City

For the last time on this journey, I adjust my watch. It's five o'clock in the morning on 30 May 2006. In Moscow, which is seven hours behind, people are still having supper on the night of the 29th.

Everyone in the carriage woke early and found it impossible to get back to sleep, not because of the motion of the train, to which we have become accustomed, but because we will shortly be arriving in Vladivostok, our final stop. We have spent the last two days in the carriage, mostly sitting round the table that has been the centre of our universe during this seemingly unending journey. We ate, told stories and I described what it felt like to plunge into Lake Baikal, although the others were more interested in our meeting with the shaman.

My publishers had a brilliant idea: they would forewarn the stations en route of our arrival time. That way, whether it was day or night, I would get out of the carriage to find people waiting on the platform with books to sign. They thanked me and I thanked them. Sometimes we stayed for only five minutes, sometimes for twenty. They blessed me and I gratefully received their blessings, which came from all kinds of people, from elderly ladies in long coats, boots and headscarves to young men who had just left work or were heading home, usually wearing only a jacket, as if to say: 'I'm too tough for the cold to get to me.'

The previous day, I had decided to walk the whole length of the train. This was something I had thought of doing several times, but always put off for another day, given that we had such a long journey ahead of us. Then I realised that we were nearly at our final destination.

I asked Yao to go with me. We opened and closed numerous doors, too many to count. Only then did I understand that I wasn't on a train, but in a city, a country, a whole universe. I should have done this before. The journey would have been so much richer; I might have met fascinating people and heard stories I could later turn into books.

I spent the whole afternoon investigating that city on wheels, only pausing to get off whenever we pulled into a station to meet any waiting readers. I walked through that great city as I have through many others and saw all the usual scenes: a man talking on his mobile phone, a boy hurrying back to fetch something he had left behind in the dining car, a mother with a baby on her lap, two young people kissing in the narrow corridor outside the compartments, oblivious to the landscape speeding past outside, radios at full blast, signs I couldn't understand, people offering and asking for things, a man with a gold tooth laughing with friends, a woman in a headscarf weeping and gazing into space. I smoked a few cigarettes with a group of people waiting by the narrow door into the next carriage, meanwhile discreetly studying those thoughtful, well-dressed men, who seemed to have the weight of the world on their shoulders.

I walked through that city, which stretched out like an ever-flowing river of steel, a city where I don't speak the local language, but what does that matter? I heard all kinds of languages and sounds and noticed that, as happens in all large cities, most people weren't talking to anyone, each passenger absorbed in his or her own problems and dreams, forced to share the same compartment with three perfect strangers, people they will never meet again and who have their own problems and dreams to contend with. However miserable or lonely they might feel, however much they would like to share their joy at some triumph or their grief at some overwhelming sadness, it's always best and safest to keep silent.

I decided to strike up a conversation with someone, a woman of about my own age. I asked if she knew what part of the country we were passing through. Yao began to translate my words, but I stopped him. I wanted to imagine what it would be like to make this journey alone. Would I have made it to the end, I wondered. The woman made a gesture indicating that she couldn't hear what I was saying above the deafening noise of the wheels on the tracks. I repeated my question, and this time she did hear, but didn't understand. She clearly thought I was slightly touched and hurriedly moved away.

I tried a second and a third person. I asked a different question: why were they travelling and what were they doing on that train? No one understood what I was asking, and I was glad in a way, because it was a pretty stupid question. They all knew what they were doing and where they were going, even I knew that, although I hadn't perhaps reached precisely the place I wanted to reach. Someone squeezing past us down the narrow corridor heard me speaking English, stopped and said very calmly:

'May I help you? Are you lost?'

'No, I'm not lost, but where exactly are we?'

'We're on the Chinese frontier and will soon be going south, down to Vladivostok.'

I thanked him and walked on. I had at least managed to have a brief conversation, which meant that it would have been possible to travel on that train alone. I would never be lost as long as there were people willing to help.

I walked through that apparently endless city and returned to the point where I had started, carrying with me the smiles, looks, kisses, music and babel of words, as well as the forest passing by outside and that I would probably never see again, although it would stay with me for ever, in my mind's eye and in my heart.

I returned to the table that has been the centre of our universe, wrote a few lines and stuck them on the mirror where Yao always put his daily thoughts.

I'm reading what I wrote yesterday after my walk through the train.

> I am not a foreigner because I haven't been praying to return safely home, I haven't wasted my time imagining my house, my desk, my side of the bed. I am not a foreigner because we are all travelling, we are all full of the same questions, the same tiredness, the same fears, the same selfishness and the same generosity. I am not a foreigner because, when I asked, I received. When I knocked, the door opened. When I looked, I found.

These, I remember, were the words of the shaman. Soon this carriage will go back where it came from. This piece of paper will disappear as soon as the cleaners arrive. But I will never forget what I wrote, because I am not and never will be a foreigner.

* * *

Hilal mostly stayed in her compartment, frantically playing her violin. Sometimes it seemed to me that she was once again talking to the angels, but at others, that she was merely practising in order to maintain her technique. On the drive back to Irkutsk, I had felt sure that I was not alone on my flight with the eagle of Baikal. Our spirits – hers and mine – had seen the same marvels.

The previous night, I had again asked if we could sleep in the same bed together. I had tried doing the ring of light exercise alone but never got anywhere, apart from making another unintended visit to the writer I had been in nineteenth-century France. He (or I) was just finishing a paragraph:

> The moments that precede sleep are very similar to death. We are filled by a torpor and it is impossible to know when the 'I' takes on a different form. Our dreams are our second life. I am incapable of going through the doors that lead us to that invisible world without a shiver.

That night, she lay by my side, I rested my head on her breast and we remained like that in silence, as if our souls had known each other for a long time and there was no need for words, only that physical contact. I finally managed to get the golden ring to take me to the very place I wanted to be: a small town outside Córdoba.

The sentence is pronounced in public, in the middle of the square, as if this were a public day of celebration. The eight girls, wearing white dresses down to their ankles, are shivering with cold, but soon they will experience the fires of Hell, lit by men who believe they are acting in the name of Heaven. I asked my superior to excuse me from being there with the other members of the Church. He did not take much persuading. I think he is still furious with me for my cowardice and glad to see the back of me. I am mingling with the crowd, feeling deeply ashamed, my head still covered by the hood of my Dominican habit.

All day, curious onlookers have been arriving from the nearby towns and, by the time dusk falls, the square is packed. The nobles sitting in the special seats reserved for them in the front row are wearing their most colourful outfits. The women have had time to arrange their hair and put on make-up so that the crowd can appreciate what they deem to be their great beauty. There is something more than just curiosity in the eyes of the people present; the most common emotion appears to be a desire for vengeance. It isn't just relief to see the guilty being punished, but glee because the guilty also happen to be the young, pretty, sensual daughters of very rich families. They deserve to be punished for having everything that most of the people there either left behind in their youth or never had at all. Let us, then, have our revenge on beauty. Let us avenge ourselves on joy, laughter and hope. There is no room in such a world for feelings that only show us up for what we are – wretched, frustrated and impotent.

The Inquisitor is holding a mass in Latin. His sermon, in which he speaks of the terrible punishments awaiting all those found guilty of heresy, is interrupted by shouts. They come from the parents of the young women about to be burned. They had been kept out of the square until then, but had managed to get in.

The Inquisitor stops his sermon, the crowd boos, and the guards go over to the interlopers and drag them away.

An ox-drawn cart arrives. The girls put their arms behind them so that their hands can be bound, and the Dominican monks then help them into the cart. The guards form a security cordon around the vehicle, the crowd moves back to let them through, and the oxen with their macabre cargo are driven towards the pyre that will be lit in a nearby field.

The girls have their heads bowed, and from where I am, I cannot know what is in their eyes, whether tears or terror. One of them was tortured so barbarously that she can only stand with the help of the others. The soldiers are having difficulty controlling the crowd now, which is laughing, hurling insults and throwing things. I see that the cart will pass close by where I am standing. I try to leave, but it's too late. The dense mass of men, women and children behind me won't allow me to move.

The cart approaches, the girls' white dresses are now stained with eggs, beer, wine and potato peelings. God have mercy on them. I hope that when the fire is lit, they ask pardon again for their sins, sins that will one day be transformed into virtues, unimaginable though that is for any of us there now. If they ask for absolution, a monk will hear their confessions once again and commend their souls to God. They will then be garrotted, and only their corpses will be burned.

If they refuse to admit their guilt, they will be burned alive.

I have witnessed other executions and sincerely hope that the girls' parents have bribed the executioner. If they have, he will pour a little oil over the wood, so that the fire burns more quickly, and the smoke will suffocate them before the flames begin to consume first their hair, then their feet, hands, face, legs and, finally, their bodies. If they have given no bribe, their daughters will burn slowly and endure indescribable pain.

The cart is now immediately in front of me. I bow my head, but one of the girls sees me. They all turn, and I prepare to be insulted and attacked as I deserve to be, for I am the guiltiest of all, the one who washed his hands of them when just one word could have changed everything.

Aleph

They call my name. The people nearby turn to look at me in surprise. Do I know these witches? Were it not for my Dominican habit, they might well attack me. A fraction of a second later, the people around me realise that I must be one of those who condemned the girls. Someone gives me a congratulatory slap on the back, and a woman says: 'Well done, you are a man of good faith.'

The girls continue calling to me. And weary of being a coward, I finally decide to raise my head and look at them.

At that point, everything freezes and I can see nothing more.

consider taking Hilal to where the Aleph is, so close by, but is that what this journey is all about? Using someone who loves me just to get an answer to a tormenting question? Will that really make me once again the king of my kingdom? If I don't find the answer now, I will find it later on. There are doubtless another three women waiting for me along my path – if I have the courage to follow it to the end. Surely I will not leave this incarnation without knowing the answer.

It's light now, and we can see the big city through the windows of the train. People get up from their seats with no show of enthusiasm, no sign that they are pleased to be arriving. Perhaps this is where our journey really begins.

The train, this city of steel, slows to a halt, this time for good. I turn to Hilal and say:

'Let's get out together.'

People are waiting on the platform. A girl with large eyes is holding up a poster bearing the Brazilian flag and some words in Portuguese. Journalists come over to me and I thank the Russian people for their kindness as I crossed their vast continent. I receive bunches of flowers, the photographers ask me to pose in front of a large bronze column topped by a two-headed eagle. There's a number engraved at the base of the column: 9,288.

There is no need to add the word 'kilometres'. Everyone who arrives here knows what that number means.

The Telephone Call

The ship is sailing calmly over the Pacific Ocean while the sun sets slowly behind the hills where the city of Vladivostok lies. The sadness I thought I saw in my travelling companions when we arrived at the station has given way to wild euphoria. We all behave as if this were the first time we had ever seen the sea. No one wants to think we'll be saying goodbye shortly and promising to meet up again soon, knowing that the purpose of this promise is simply to make parting easier.

The journey is coming to a close, the adventure is about to end, and in three days' time, we will all be going back to our respective houses, where we will embrace our families, see our children, read through the correspondence that has accumulated in our absence, show off the hundreds of photos we've taken, tell our stories about the train, the cities we passed through and the people we met along the way.

And all to convince ourselves that the journey really did happen. In another three days' time, once we're back in our daily routine, it will feel as if we had never left and never made that long journey. We have the photos,

Aleph

the tickets, the souvenirs, but time – the only, absolute, eternal master of our lives – will be telling us: you never left this house, this room, this computer.

Two weeks? What's that in a whole lifetime? Nothing has changed in the street, the neighbours are still gossiping about the same old things, the newspaper you bought this morning carries exactly the same news: the World Cup about to start in Germany, the debate over whether Iran should be allowed to have nuclear weapons, the Israeli–Palestinian conflict, the latest celebrity scandal, the constant complaints about things the government promised to do, but hasn't.

No, nothing has changed. But we – who went off in search of our kingdom and discovered lands we had never seen before – we know we are different. However, the more we try to explain, the more we will persuade ourselves that this journey, like all the others, only exists in our memory. Perhaps we will tell our grandchildren about it or even write a book on the subject, but what exactly will we say?

Nothing, or perhaps only what happened outside, not what changed inside.

We may never see each other again. And the only person with her eyes fixed on the horizon now is Hilal. She must be thinking about how to resolve this problem. No, for her, the Trans-Siberian railway doesn't end here. Yet she doesn't show her feelings, and when someone talks to her, she replies kindly and politely, something she has never done for as long as we've known each other.

Yao tries to strike up a conversation with her. He has already made a couple of attempts, but she always moves away after exchanging only a few words. In the end, he gives up and comes to join me.

'What can I do?'

'Just respect her silence.'

'Yes, I agree, but …'

'I know. Meanwhile, try thinking about yourself for a change. Remember what the shaman said: you killed God. If you don't take this opportunity to bring Him back to life, this journey will have been a waste of time. I know a lot of people who help others simply as a way of avoiding their own problems.'

Yao pats me on the back, as if to say 'I understand', then leaves me alone to gaze out to sea.

Now that I've reached the furthest point in my journey, I once again sense my wife by my side. That afternoon, I met some more readers, we had the usual party, I visited the local prefect, and, for the first time in my life, held in my hands a real Kalashnikov, the one the prefect keeps in his office. As we were leaving, I noticed the newspaper lying on his desk. I don't understand a word of Russian, but the photos spoke for themselves: football.

Aleph

The World Cup is due to start in a few days' time! She's waiting for me in Munich, where we will meet very shortly. I'll tell her how much I've missed her and describe in detail what happened between me and Hilal.

She'll say: 'Please, I've heard this story four times already', and we'll go out for a drink at some German bierkeller.

I didn't make this journey in order to find the words missing from my life, but to be the king of my own world again. And it's here; I'm back in touch with myself and with the magical universe all around me.

Yes, I could have reached the same conclusions without ever leaving Brazil, but just like Santiago, the shepherd boy in one of my books, sometimes you have to travel a long way in order to find what is near. When the rain returns to earth, it brings with it the things of the air. The magical and the extraordinary are with me and with everyone in the Universe all the time, but sometimes we forget that and need to be reminded, even if we have to cross the largest continent in the world from one side to the other. We return laden down with treasures that might end up getting buried again, and then we will have to set off once more in search of them. That's what makes life interesting – believing in treasures and in miracles.

'Let's celebrate. Is there any vodka on the boat?'

No, there isn't, and Hilal fixes me with angry eyes.

'Celebrate what? The fact that I'm going to be stuck here alone until I get the train all the way back and spend endless days and nights thinking about everything we've been through together?'

'No, I need to celebrate what I've just experienced, to raise a glass to myself. And you need to toast your courage. You set off in search of adventure and you found it. You might be sad for a while, but someone is sure to light a fire on a nearby mountain. You'll see the light, go towards it and find the man you've been looking for all your life. You're young and, you know, I sensed last night that it wasn't your hands playing the violin, but the hands of God. Let God use your hands. You *will* be happy, even if right now you feel only despair.'

'You have absolutely no idea what I'm feeling. You're just an egotist, who thinks the world owes you something. I gave myself to you entirely and yet here I am again, being left high and dry.'

There's no point arguing, but I know she's right. That's how it will be. I'm fifty-nine and she's twenty-one.

We go back to the place where we're staying. Not a hotel this time, but a vast house built in 1974 for a summit on disarmament between Leonid Brezhnev, then Secretary-General of the Communist Party of the Soviet Union, and the American president of the time, Gerald Ford. It is made all of white marble, with a vast hall in the middle and a series of rooms leading off it. These must once have been intended for political delegations, but are now used for occasional guests.

We intend having a shower, changing our clothes and then going straight out to supper in the city, far from that chilly atmosphere. However, a man is standing right in the middle of the hall. My publishers go over to him. Yao and I keep a prudent distance.

The man takes out his mobile phone and dials a number. Now my publisher is speaking respectfully into the phone, his eyes bright with happiness. My editor is smiling too. My publisher's voice echoes round the marble walls.

'What's going on?' I ask.

'You'll find out in a minute,' answers Yao.

My publisher turns off the phone and comes towards me, beaming.

'We're going back to Moscow tomorrow,' he says. 'We have to be there by five in the afternoon.'

'Weren't we going to stay here for a couple of days? I haven't even had time for a wander round the city. Besides, it's a nine-hour flight to Moscow. How could we possibly be there by five o'clock?'

'There's a seven-hour time difference. If we leave here at midday, we'll be there by two. That's plenty of time. I'm going to cancel the restaurant booking this evening and ask them to serve supper here. I've got a lot of arranging to do.'

'But why the urgency? My plane for Germany leaves on—'

He interrupts me, saying:

'It seems that President Vladimir Putin has read all about your journey and would like to meet you.'

The Soul of Turkey

'And what about me?'

My publisher turns to Hilal.

'It was your decision to come with us and you can go back how and when you want. It's nothing to do with us.'

The man with the mobile phone has vanished. My publishers leave, and Yao goes with them. Hilal and I are alone in the middle of that vast, oppressive marble hallway.

Everything happened so fast that we still haven't recovered from the shock. I had no idea President Putin even knew about my journey. Hilal cannot believe that things are going to end so abruptly, so suddenly, without her having another opportunity to talk to me of love, to explain how important everything we've experienced is for our lives and that we should carry on even if I am married. That, at least, is what I imagine is going through her mind.

'YOU CAN'T DO THIS TO ME! YOU CAN'T JUST LEAVE ME HERE! YOU KILLED ME ONCE BECAUSE YOU DIDN'T HAVE THE GUTS TO SAY "NO", AND NOW YOU'RE GOING TO KILL ME AGAIN!'

She runs to her room, and I fear the worst. If she's serious, anything is possible. I want to phone my publisher and ask him to buy a ticket for her; otherwise, we could be faced by a terrible tragedy, and then there will be no meeting with Putin, no kingdom, no redemption, no conquest, and my big adventure will end in suicide and death. I run to her room, which is on the second floor, but she has already opened the windows.

'Stop! You won't kill yourself if you jump from this height, you'll just be crippled for the rest of your life.'

She isn't listening. I have to stay calm and in control of the situation. I have to be as authoritative as she was at Baikal, when she ordered me not to turn round and see her naked. A thousand thoughts go through my mind, and I take the easiest route.

'Look, I love you. I would never leave you here alone.'

She knows this isn't true, but my words of love have an instantaneous effect.

'You love me like a river, you said, but I love you the way a woman loves a man.'

Hilal doesn't want to die. If she did, she would have said nothing. But quite apart from the words she used, her voice is saying: 'You're part of me, the most important part, and it's being left behind. I will never be the person I was.' She's quite wrong, but this is not the moment to explain something she won't understand.

'And I love you the way a man loves a woman, as I did before and always will for as long as the world exists. I explained to you once: time doesn't pass. Do I have to say it again?'

She turns round.

'That's a lie. Life is a dream from which we only wake when we meet death. Time passes while we live. I'm a musician and I have to deal with the time of musical notation every day. If time didn't exist, there would be no music.'

She's speaking coherently now. And I do love her. Not as a woman, but I do love her.

'Music isn't a succession of notes. It's the constant movement of a note between sound and silence,' I say.

'What do you know about music? Even if you were right, what does it matter now? You're a prisoner of your past, and so am I. If I loved you in one life, I will continue to love you for ever! I have no heart, no body, no soul, nothing! All I have is love. You think I exist, but that's just an optical illusion. What you're seeing is Love in its purest state, yearning to reveal itself, but there is no time or space where it can do that.'

She moves away from the window and starts pacing up and down the room. She has no intention of throwing herself out of the window now. Apart from her footsteps on the wooden floor, all I can hear is the infernal tick-tock of a clock, proving me wrong about time. Time does exist and, at that very moment, it is busily consuming us. I need Yao, that poor man, through whose soul the black wind of loneliness still blows, but who always feels good whenever he can help someone else; he could have calmed her down.

'Go back to your wife! Go back to the woman who has always been by your side through thick and thin! She's generous, loving, tolerant, and I'm everything you hate: complicated, aggressive, obsessive, capable of anything!'

'What right have you to talk about my wife?'

I am once again losing control of the situation.

'I'll say what I like. You never could control me and you never will!'

Keep calm. Keep talking and she'll quieten down. But I've never seen anyone in such a state before. I try another tack:

'Then be glad that no one can control you. Celebrate the fact that you were brave enough to risk your career and set off in search of adventure, and find it too. Remember what I said on the boat: someone, one day, will light the sacred fire for you. And from now on, it won't be *your* fingers playing the violin, but the angels'. Let God use your hands. Your feelings of bitterness will eventually disappear, and the person fate has placed in your path will arrive bearing a bouquet of happiness in his hands, and then everything will be fine. Right now, you feel desperate and think I'm lying, but that's how it will be.'

Too late.

I have said precisely the wrong thing, which could be summarised in just two words: 'Grow up.' No woman

I've ever known would have accepted that piece of advice.

Hilal picks up a heavy metal lamp, rips the plug out of the wall, and hurls the lamp in my direction. I manage to catch it before it hits my face, but now she's slapping me as hard as she can. I drop the lamp and try to grab her arms, but fail. A fist hits my nose, and blood spurts in all directions.

She and I are covered in my blood.

The soul of Turkey will give your husband all the love she possesses, but she will spill his blood before she reveals what it is she is seeking.

'Right, come with me!'

My tone of voice has changed completely. She stops hitting me. I take her by the arm and drag her out of the room.

'Come with me!'

There's no time for explanations. I run down the stairs, taking with me a Hilal who is now more frightened than angry. My heart is pounding. We hurry out of the building. The car that was supposed to be taking me to supper is still waiting.

'To the train station!'

The driver looks at me uncomprehendingly. I open the door, shove Hilal inside, then get in after her.

'Tell him to go straight to the train station!'

She repeats my words in Russian, and the driver obeys.

'Tell him to ignore any speed limits. I'll make it all right with him afterwards. We need to get there fast!'

The man seems to like what he hears. He races off, tyres squealing on every bend, and other cars brake when they spot the car's official insignia. To my surprise, he has a siren, which he places on the roof. My fingers are digging into Hilal's arm.

'You're hurting me!' she says.

I relax the pressure. I'm praying, asking God to help me, to make sure I arrive in time and that everything is where it should be.

Hilal is talking to me, begging me to calm down, apologising for acting the way she did, saying that she hadn't really intended killing herself, that it was all an act. No one who truly loves someone would destroy them or themselves, and she would never let me spend another incarnation suffering and blaming myself for what had happened – once was enough. I would like to be able to respond, but I'm not really following what she's saying.

Ten minutes later, the car screeches to a halt outside the train station.

I open the door, drag Hilal out of the car and into the station, where we find the barrier to the platform closed. I try to push my way through, only to see two massive guards hove into view. Hilal leaves me alone for a moment, and for the first time during that whole journey, I feel lost, unsure of how to proceed. I need her by my side. Without her, nothing, absolutely nothing will be possible. I sit down on the ground. The men look at my blood-spattered face and clothes. They come over and gesture to me to get up, then start asking questions. I try to explain that I don't speak Russian, but they become increasingly aggressive. Other people begin to gather round to see what's going on.

Hilal reappears with the driver. He doesn't raise his voice, but what he says to the guards brings about a complete change of attitude. I have no time to lose. There's something I must do. The guards push the onlookers aside. The way ahead is now free. I take Hilal's hand and we walk onto the platform, run down to the end, where everything is in darkness. In the gloom, I can just make out the last carriage.

Yes, it's still there!

I put my arms around Hilal while I recover my breath. My heart is beating furiously from the physical effort and from the adrenaline coursing through my veins. I feel slightly dizzy. I didn't have much to eat at lunchtime, but I mustn't faint now. The soul of Turkey will show me what I need to see. Hilal is stroking me as if I were her child, telling me to calm down, she's there by my side and no harm will come to me.

I breathe deeply, and my pulse gradually returns to normal.

'Come with me.'

The door is open. No one would dare get on a train in Russia in order to steal anything. We enter the carriage. I make her stand with her back against the wall in the vestibule, as I had at the very beginning of that endless journey. Our faces are very close, as if the next step will be a kiss. A distant light, perhaps from a lamp on another platform, is reflected in her eyes.

And even though we're in complete darkness, she and I will be able to see. This is where the Aleph is. Time suddenly changes frequency, and we're propelled at speed down a dark tunnel. She knows what's happening now, and so won't be frightened.

'Take my hand, and let's go together into the other world, NOW!'

Camels and deserts appear, rains and winds, the fountain in a village in the Pyrenees, the waterfall at the Monasterio de Piedra, the Irish coast, a corner of a street in what looks like London, women on motorbikes, a prophet standing at the foot of the sacred mountain, the cathedral in Santiago de Compostela, prostitutes waiting for clients in Geneva, witches dancing naked round a fire, a man preparing to shoot his wife and her lover, the steppes of some country in Asia, where a woman is weaving beautiful tapestries while she waits for her man to return, mad people in a hospital, the seas with all their fish and the Universe with each and every star. The sound of babies being born, old men dying, cars braking, women singing, men cursing and doors, doors and more doors.

Aleph

I go through all the lives I have lived, will live and am living. I'm a man in a train with a woman, a writer in mid nineteenth-century France, I am the many people I was and will be. We go through the door I want to go through. The hand I am holding disappears.

Around me, a crowd smelling of beer and wine are guffawing and shouting and hurling insults.

emale voices are calling to me. I feel ashamed, I don't want to look at them, but the voices insist. Other people in the crowd compliment me: So I was the person responsible, was I? Saving the town from heresy and sin! The girls' voices continue to call my name.

I have been cowardly enough to last me for the rest of my life. I slowly raise my head.

The cart has almost passed by; another second and I would hear nothing more. But now I am looking at them. Despite the humiliations they have been through, they seem quite serene, as if they had matured, grown up, married and had children, and were now calmly heading for death, the fate of all human beings. They struggled while they could, but at some point they must have understood that this was their fate, set down long before they were born. Only two things can reveal life's great secrets: suffering and love. They have experienced both.

And that is what I saw in their eyes: love. We had played together at being princes and princesses, made plans for the future as all children do. Life decided to separate us. I chose to serve God, and they followed a different path.

I am nineteen, slightly older than the girls now gazing gratefully down at me because I have finally deigned to look at them. A great weight lies on my soul, though, a weight full of contradictions and guilt at never having had the courage to say 'No', and all in the name of an absurd sense of obedience, which I would like to believe was true and logical.

The girls are still looking at me, and that second lasts an eternity. One of them again calls out my name. I move my lips silently so that only they can understand:

'Forgive me.'

'There's no need,' one of them says. 'We talked with the spirits, and they revealed to us what would happen. The time for fear is past, now there is only the time of hope. Are we guilty? One day, the world will judge us and we will not be the ones to feel ashamed. We will meet again in the future, when your life and work will be dedicated to those who are so sorely misunderstood today. Your voice will speak out loudly and many will listen to you.'

The cart is moving off, and I start to run along beside it, despite being pushed away by the guards.

'Love will conquer hatred,' says another of the girls, speaking as calmly as if we were still in the forests and woods of our childhood. 'When the time comes, those who are burned today will be exalted. Wizards and alchemists will return, the Goddess will be welcomed and witches celebrated. And all for the greatness of God. That is the blessing we place on your head now, until the end of time.'

A guard punches me in the stomach, and I double up, all the breath knocked out of me, but still I keep looking at the girls. The cart is moving past me now, and I won't be able to catch it again.

push Hilal away. We are back on the train.

'I couldn't see clearly,' she says. 'It looked like a crowd shouting, and there was a man wearing a hood. I think it was you, but I'm not sure.'

'Don't worry.'

'Did you get the answer you needed?'

I would like to say: 'Yes, I finally understood my destiny', but my voice is choked with tears.

'You won't leave me alone in this city, will you?'

I put my arms around her.

'Of course I won't.'

Moscow, 1 June 2006

That night, when we return to the hotel, Yao is there waiting for Hilal with a return ticket to Moscow. We will fly back on the same plane, although in different classes. My publishers cannot accompany me to my audience with Vladimir Putin, but a journalist friend of mine has permission to do so.

When the plane lands, Hilal and I leave by different exits. I am led into a special room, where two men and my friend are waiting. I ask to go to the terminal where the other passengers are disembarking, saying that I need to say goodbye to someone. One of the men says there isn't time, but my friend points out that it's only two in the afternoon, and the meeting isn't until five. And even if the president were waiting for me at the house outside Moscow where he's usually to be found at this time of year, it will only take us, at most, fifty minutes to get there.

'Besides, if there's any problem, your cars are fitted with sirens, aren't they?' he says jokingly.

We make our way to the other terminal. I enter a florist's and buy a dozen roses. We reach the arrivals gate, which is crowded with people waiting for friends and relatives arriving from far-flung places.

'Does anyone here understand English?' I shout.

People look startled, doubtless because of the three burly men with me.

'Does anyone speak English?'

A few hands are raised. I show them the bouquet of roses.

'A young woman whom I love very much will be arriving shortly. I need eleven volunteers to help me give her these flowers.'

Eleven volunteers immediately appear by my side. We form a queue. Hilal comes out of the main door, sees me, smiles and heads straight for me. One by one the volunteers hand her the roses. She looks half-confused and half-happy. When she finally reaches me, I hand her the twelfth rose and fold her in the warmest of embraces.

'Aren't you going to tell me you love me?' she asks, trying to keep control of the situation.

'Yes. I love you like a river. But now we must say goodbye.'

'Goodbye?' she says with a laugh. 'You're not going to get rid of me that easily.'

The two men waiting to take me to see the president, say something in Russian. My journalist friend laughs. I ask him what they said, but Hilal herself translates:

'They said it's the most romantic thing they've ever seen in this airport.'

St George's Day, 2010

Author's note

I met Hilal again in September 2006, when I invited her to take part in a conference at the Monastery of Melk in Austria. We travelled from there to Barcelona, then on to Pamplona and Burgos. It was in one of those cities that she told me she had left music school and given up playing the violin. I tried to convince her to think again, but something inside told me that she, too, had become queen of her world again and needed to rule over her own realm.

While I was writing this book, Hilal sent me two emails saying that she had dreamed I was writing about what had happened between us. I asked her to be patient, and only told her about the book when I had finished writing it. She didn't appear in the least surprised.

I wonder if I was right to think that if I missed that opportunity with Hilal, I would have another three chances (after all, eight girls were to be executed that day, and I had already met five of them). I doubt now that I will ever know: of the eight girls condemned to death, only one really loved me, the girl whose name I never knew.

I no longer work with Lena, Yuri Smirnov and the Sofia Publishing House, but I would like to thank them for the unique experience of travelling across Russia by train.

The prayer of forgiveness used by Hilal in Novosibirsk is one that has already been channelled by other people. When I say in the book that I had heard it before in Brazil, I am referring to the spirit of André Luiz, a little boy.

Finally, I would like to warn against the use of the ring of light exercise. As I mentioned earlier, any return to the past with no knowledge of the process can have dramatic and disastrous consequences.

Life is a
journey

Make sure you don't miss a thing.
Live it with Paulo Coelho.

What are you searching for?

A transforming journey on the pilgrims' road to Santiago – and the first of Paulo's extraordinary books.

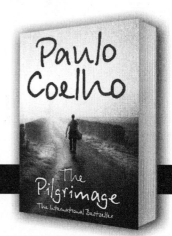

The Pilgrimage

Do you believe in yourself?

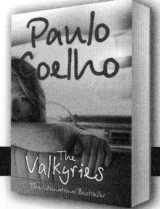

A modern-day adventure in the searing heat of the Mojave desert and an exploration of fear and self-doubt.

The Valkyries

How can you find your heart's desire?

A world-wide phenomenon; an inspiration for anyone seeking their path in life.

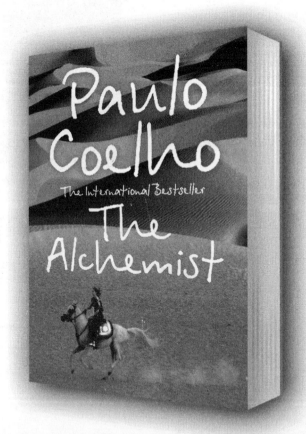

The Alchemist

Could you be tempted into evil?

The inhabitants of a small town are challenged by a mysterious stranger to choose between good and evil.

The Devil and Miss Prym

Can faith triumph over suffering?

Paulo's brilliant telling of the story of Elijah, who was forced to choose between love and duty.

The Fifth Mountain

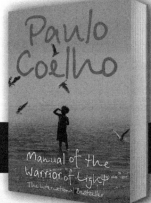

Can we dare to be true to ourselves?

A story that will transform the way we think about love, joy and sacrifice.

How will you know who your soulmate is?

A moving tale of passion, mystery and spirituality.

What happens when obsession turns to murder?

An entralling story of jealousy,
death and suspense.

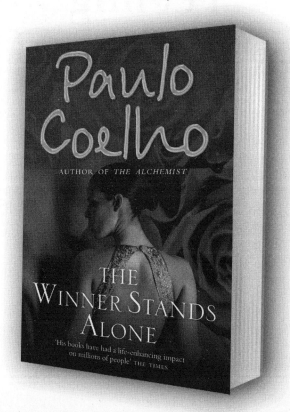

The Winner Stands Alone

Feeling
inspired?

Discover more about the
world of Paulo Coelho.